Texas Marvel

To Elizabeth and Sarah Branigan — two real Texans. You are special!

Rita Kerr

1-25-90

Rita Kerr

Eakin Press ★ Austin, Texas

Stories For Young Americans Series

FIRST EDITION

Copyright © 1987
By Rita Kerr

Published in the United States of America
By Eakin Press, P. O. Box 23069, Austin, Texas 78735

ISBN 0-89015-597-6

Library of Congress Cataloging-in-Publication Data

Kerr, Rita.
  Texas marvel.

  Summary: Fictionalized boyhood adventures of Doctor Marvel Sellers, an early Texas pioneer, and his family in the nineteenth century.
  [1. Texas—Fiction. 2. Frontier and pioneer life—Texas—Fiction] I. Title.
PZ7.K468458Tar 1987 [Fic] 87-5435
ISBN 0-89015-597-6 (pbk.)

This book is dedicated to the memory of Marvel Sellers, early Texas pioneer, and to the many students of Elma Neal Elementary School in San Antonio.

Contents

Preface

The story of *Texas Marvel* is fiction based on historical facts. In the early 1860s, Dr. John Sellers and his boys, Melton and Marvel, started on a hundred-mile trip in a covered wagon from Center Point, Texas, to Goliad. They had many exciting adventures before the boys were captured by Indians.

In later years, Marvel Sellers became a doctor. He often told of his experiences with the Indians. This book, *Texas Marvel*, is based on those experiences.

Acknowledgments

The author wishes to thank Susan Stone, granddaughter of Dr. Marvel Sellers, for her suggestions in the writing of this book. Special thanks goes to Kevin McGown, Jimmy and Larry Kerr, and to the teachers and students of Elma Neal Elementary School who critiqued the first draft of *Texas Marvel*.

The author also expresses her thanks to the following librarians and friends for their encouragement and interest in her work: Ruth McConnell, Peggy Litherbury, Laura Edwards, and Dee Dee Burch.

Last, but not least, the author wishes to thank her co-worker and partner, Larry Kerr.

1

The Surprise

"Pa, are you sure this is the wagon my Dad was driving when the Injuns killed him?" Melton's blue eyes were serious.

"I am sure," Pa Sellers replied. His arms rested lightly around Melton, and his own son, Marvel. "Ten years ago today we found your Dad on that very seat. He was dead with an Injun's arrow through his heart!"

"And my Mama, where was she?" Melton's voice was scarcely above a whisper as he asked the question and stared at the weatherworn wagon. The tattered covering flapped in the gentle breeze.

Pa replied soberly, "Your Mama was on the floor back there. You were a little fellow sleeping in a basket at her side. Son, your Mama was dying, poor soul. She was burning with fever when she begged us to take you." He tenderly patted the boy's arm. "Of course, we told her that we would. She smiled and took her last breath. We buried your folks beside the trail. That was all we could do. We brought this wagon on to Texas with us. It has been standing here ever since. And you? You've been like our own little boy for ten years now."

The taller of the boys had listened quietly while he studied the rusty wagon wheels. When his father paused, Marvel asked, "How old was I?"

"You were just a little shaver, Marvel, learning how to walk!"

"Why did you decide to be a doctor? Why did you come to Center Point anyway?" The tale was one of Marvel's favorites.

Pa laughed. "One thing at a time, son." When he squatted, the boys knew it was Pa's signal that a story was coming. They squatted, too.

"Well," he began, "back in the 1820s times were different. In those days the women folks had to know a lot about treating sicknesses with herbs and plants. That was all the medicine they had. For as long as I can remember I've had a way with animals — especially sick ones. When my Ma saw my interest, she taught me some about curing with herbs. My brothers Saul and Jack nicknamed me 'Doctor John' when I was a little tot, and I've been called that ever since. Of course later, when I grew up and went to school, I became a real 'Doctor John.'"

Marvel spoke up, "You can call me 'Doc.' I'm going to be a doctor, too, when I grow up."

Pa rumpled his son's curls and teased, "Doc? Well, one thing you need to learn is that a wise man always listens. That's how we heard about Texas and decided to come here. After we three Sellers boys got married we naturally wanted children and a place of our own. The more we heard about Texas the more excited we got. We talked it over with our wives. They liked the idea of coming to Texas and were eager to get started. We packed everything into our wagons and set out. We met some mighty friendly folks who offered us seeds and tools they could spare. We took them! Before we got here we had chickens and a couple of cows. We must have been a sight with all that stuff."

Melton giggled. "Glory, I wish I could have seen you."

Pa had a faraway look in his eyes. "By late February we had reached Louisiana, and that was when the fun began."

Marvel smiled. He knew what was coming.

"Son, you were born first. And while we were waiting for your Ma to get stronger, my brother Saul's wife had a baby girl! Then Jack's little John was born. They named him John after me."

"Mercy," Melton mumbled. "Three babies!"

"That was why we nicknamed that spring of 1849 the 'Birthing Spring.' We soon learned that traveling in a wagon with little ones wasn't easy. The wet weather didn't help much either. We would travel a few weeks, then stop so the women could rest and wash the clothes. After a few days we would start out again. When folks along the way heard where we were going, they sent messages by us to their friends and families living in Texas. We made a heap of friends that way."

Pa pushed the hair from his eyes and went on. "Most everybody we talked to said we ought to settle in Goliad. My brothers decided to go there to find land. But me and your Ma dreamed of a nice place on the river and lots of trees so that you children could fish and hunt. We kept looking until we found the right spot. We liked the land along the Pedernales River but, when we heard they needed a doctor in Center Point, we came here. We have been here ever since."

"Your brothers went on to Goliad?"

Pa nodded.

"How long has it been since you saw your brothers, Pa?"

"Too long, Marvel. Ten years! But now that there is another doctor in Center Point, we're going to change that. I've decided to take a little vacation. Me and you boys are going to Goliad!"

"Goliad!" The two voices became one. "We're going to Goliad? When?"

"We will leave before sunrise day after tomorrow."
Pa chuckled and stood up. "We have lots to do before then."

Marvel's thoughts were in a spin. "How long will we stay? Won't Ma need us?"

Pa's hand rested on the boy's shoulder. "You are right. We've got to be back before the new baby comes. Ma will need us then. Rachel Smith and her husband are coming to help Ma with the little ones until we get back."

Melton's eyes glistened with excitement. "Are we going on horses?"

"No, son, Goliad is too far. Besides, you would be worn out in no time riding a horse. Your legs are too short for a saddle—even if you had a saddle, which you don't. The oxen will pull the wagon."

The older boy moaned in disgust. "Oh, Pa, old Cain and Abel are so slow. Horses could go faster."

Pa's long legs headed for the house. The boys ran to keep up. "That's true, but Injuns don't take oxen. They like horses."

The boys stopped in their tracks. Their mouths flew open in surprise. "Injuns? What Injuns?"

Pa chuckled. "I don't know—Comanches, maybe Apaches. I understand that they are unhappy having to live on reservations. I can't say I blame them, but don't you go talking to Ma about Injuns or she won't let us go."

Dr. John Sellers glanced around his place. His eyes came to rest on the house. "I love this land. It has been good to us. It was a fine day when we decided to settle here."

Like most of the homes around Center Point, theirs had a rock foundation. The twin cabins were joined by a rough shingled roof with a breezeway porch between. One cabin was the family's sleeping quarters and the other was the kitchen. Pa's two latest additions were a storage shed for food and supplies; the other shed was for their animals.

As they stepped onto the porch they saw Ma through the open doorway. Marvel could contain himself no longer. He raced into the kitchen shouting, "Ma, we're going to Goliad, to Goliad!"

Melton sang out, "We're going in the wagon to see Pa's brothers!"

The kitchen's silence was shattered. The three younger Sellers children screamed, "I want to go! I want to go!" The dog added to the confusion by barking wildly.

"Children! Children, hush!" Ma scolded. "And put that dog outside. Now, stop screaming or the neighbors will think something is wrong."

"Aw, shucks, come on Rags. Out!" Marvel grumbled to his dog.

"And watch your English. You, too, Dr. John Sellers. You all sound like you came from the backwoods somewhere. Now, go wash your hands—the bunch of you. Dinner is ready, so hurry up. Don't you leave a mess at the washstand."

The smaller children awaited their turns and listened in stunned silence while their brothers talked about the trip. A short time later they took their places on the benches. The two chairs at either end of the long table were reserved for their parents. The kitchen, which was usually quiet, was now alive with a feeling of excitement. Everyone tried to eat and talk at once. Between mouthfuls of turnip greens and thick, buttered corn bread the children asked questions.

Marvel hoped to learn something about their trip. He asked, "How long will it take us to get to Goliad?"

Pa rubbed his whiskered chin, rolling his eyes thoughtfully. "I don't rightly know. It may take a couple of weeks, maybe less, depending on the roads and creeks. I understand that the trails to the shingle and sawmill camps on the other side of Center Point are in fair shape. Other roads are bad. And, of course, the oxen are slow."

"Which way will you go, John?"

"Honey, I have been talking to folks who have been to Goliad. They say the best way is go east along the Guadalupe River. Then—at Gonzales—turn south. We will follow the river most of the way. They say we can't get lost, but I think I will make us a map." He paused to catch his breath. With a devilish twinkle in his eyes, he added, "I need supplies and medicines. So, coming back we will head northwest—through San Antonio!"

The younger Seller children repeated the word, "San Antonio?"

Just as most Texans did, the family felt a close kinship with the famous heroes who had fought and died at the Alamo in 1836 to help Texas win freedom from Mexico. They delighted in stories of the Texan's final victory at the Battle of San Jacinto. It was no secret that they dreamed of someday seeing the spot where the little band of brave men had fought so gallantly. They felt sure that San Antonio must be the most important city in the world.

In an awed whisper, Marvel asked, "San Antonio? The place where Davy Crockett died?"

Melton formed the words slowly, "The Alamo? Will we see where James Bowie was killed?"

There was a starry look in Pa's eyes. "We will see it all—the Alamo, the walls—everything! But first, boys, you must finish eating. Then we will take a look at the wagon."

"I'm done!" The table shook. Dishes rattled. Milk from the pitcher splashed onto the table as the boys leaped to their feet.

"Boys! Slow down! See what you did?" Ma scolded. "And look at you, John! You are as excited as those two boys!"

With a downcast expression, Pa walked over and patted her arm. "We didn't mean any harm." His eyes searched hers. "Are you all right, honey?"

Her pretty face softened. She laughed, "I will feel better when you three are on your way. Then I will have some peace. Now, go and see about your precious wagon. Be gone with you and give me some rest."

The children raced out the door after their father. The sound of their footsteps and voices faded into the distance. Ma Sellers sighed and closed her eyes, absorbing the hushed silence of her kitchen. A sudden movement of her unborn child made her wonder what might lie ahead for them.

2

Off to Goliad

Two mornings later, as the first pink rays of the sun crept into the April sky, John Sellers made a final check of the wagon. The pots and pans needed for their journey were at the rear of the wagon. Their food supply was nearby. Ma had cooked enough corn bread, sausage, and beans and other things to last them for several days. She knew that the boys—especially Melton—were always hungry.

The wagon floor behind the driver's seat was piled high with sacks of seeds, jars of wild honey, and bars of lye soap. Those were going to Pa's brothers in Goliad. Most of the things had been payment from Pa's patients. Few people had money; they paid for his services with what they had. Pa knew his family would never go hungry as long as folks gave him eggs and meat for his doctoring. Their dog, Rags, had been payment for delivering twin boys to the Smiths.

"Well," Pa said, "I guess we are ready."

The boys ran to kiss their mother and their brother and sisters. They raced for the wagon, wishing again that the wagon bed was lower to the ground or that their legs were longer. Once they were settled on the seat, Ma handed them her favorite quilt and smiled. "You tuck this around you. It is chilly this morning."

"Thanks, honey . . ."

Pa could not finish because of Marvel's screams. "Pa! I forgot my dog! We can't go without my dog. He has to go. Oh, please, Pa. Can't he go with us!"

Melton shook his finger knowingly in his father's direction. "We had better take him. You remember how ornery Rags can be when he doesn't get his way? I bet he will howl and whine the whole time we are gone. Ma wouldn't get any rest or peace because of that dog. You had better let him come along, Pa."

Ma did not give her husband a chance to open his mouth. "John Sellers, you take that dog! I will have my hands full with these three children. Melton is right — I don't need that pesky dog howling all the time you are gone."

Laughing softly, Pa lifted the shaggy black-and-white dog into Marvel's outstretched arms and winked. "All right. I know when I'm beat." The animal's rough tongue licked Pa's cheek. He complained loudly. "Stop that!"

Turning to the smaller children standing by their mother, Pa kissed each one of them. Then he turned to his wife, took her in his arms, and kissed her on the mouth. Tenderly patting her back he whispered, "I love you, hon. Take care of yourself."

Pa crawled up beside the boys. With the first signs of day they were off.

"Giddy-up, Cain and Abel," Pa called loudly.

The oxen responded to his command. The wagon squeaked in protest. Marvel swallowed the lump in his throat when he waved to the children clinging to their mother's apron.

It was impossible to hear their final farewells because of Rags's barking. The boys waved their hats until the house faded into the murky shadows.

Rags snuggled between them under the quilt to await

9

the break of day. Marvel sighed loudly, "Just think — we are on our way to Goliad!"

"Glory," Melton said. "I can't believe we are really going."

They gradually grew accustomed to the wagon's swaying over the uneven ground. They searched for telltale chimney smoke, but the houses grew fewer and farther apart. When the sun slowly peeked up over the eastern horizon, they saw unfamiliar sights. The boys gaped in wonder, pointing to first one thing and then another.

"Pa, everything looks different — even the trees," Melton declared. "And look!"

He pointed to two long-eared rabbits which had appeared from the weeds to race ahead of the oxen. When Rags saw them, he frantically tried to get out of the wagon.

"No, Rags, sit still," Marvel scolded, trying to hold the wiggling animal back. "Oh, Pa, he wants one of those rabbits. Can't we get down and try to catch one for him?"

His father smiled at the idea. "You can try, but you boys be careful not to fall into a chug hole." Rags disappeared into the weeds when his paws touched the ground. The boys walked beside the wagon at first. Suddenly, one of the floppy-eared rabbits reappeared in the road. Rags was right behind it. The chase was on, with Rags and the boys in hot pursuit of the rabbit. The boys screamed and yelled. When the rabbit increased the speed of his great rocking leaps, he left them far behind in a cloud of dust.

From his seat in the wagon, Pa watched the race. He laughed so hard that tears ran down his cheek as he watched the hunters try in vain to catch the rabbit. The chase was hopeless. "Better come on back now, boys. You lost the race."

Rags did not want to return to the wagon. Only Marvel's arms convinced him that he had no choice. Huffing and puffing from the run, they crawled back into their places.

"What kind of rabbit was that anyway. Pa?"

"It was a jack rabbit! Funny thing about those rabbits — they change colors. They are gray in the summer and sometimes white in the winter. We will probably see a lot of them along the way."

"You hear that, Rags?" Marvel said. "You may get another chance to catch one." Rags wagged his tail and barked.

Each passing mile brought more of nature's wonders: a herd of deer, a hawk circling high overhead, a bubbling spring, a patch of brightly colored flowers. Pa agreed with the boys. The world seemed suddenly alive and new.

3

Two Strangers

"I must have spring fever," Pa exclaimed with a yawn. "No doubt about it, spring is the best time to make a trip like this. Things are just turning green, and it's not as hot as it would be in the summer. Look, there are some of Ma's favorite flowers—those bluebonnets. It isn't often you see yellow and white ones like that. Usually, there are only blue ones. Each year they bloom, drop their seeds, and die to come again the next spring. That is the way it was planned to be. Spring brings new life everywhere—in the trees, in the earth, and in the water. New life means new hope to all living things."

Melton asked shyly, "Is that why most baby animals are born in the spring, Pa?"

"Yes, son," Pa answered slowly. "Spring brings all kinds of new babies to our world. Life is ever-changing. Speaking of new things, son, I reckon it's about time you learned to drive the wagon. Do you want to try?"

Marvel did not bother to answer. Instead, he reached for the reins that guided the team. He had dreamed of the day when he would drive the wagon. He had often thought as he watched his father that it did not seem hard to do.

"Giddy-up, Cain and Abel," he called. The oxen plodded slowly on, never knowing or caring who was in command. With each mile Marvel felt more confident and sure of himself. Sometime later he glanced at his father and said, "Couldn't Melton have a try? It's not hard. He can do it, Pa."

"I reckon so, son."

Melton felt ten feet tall as he took the reins. Pa chuckled to himself as he thought of how important the boy must feel. But, when the oxen stumbled in the deep ruts, he said, "I had better take over. The ground should be smoother over on those weeds."

He was right. The oxen settled back into their steady pace once the wagon rolled over onto the tender grasses.

Marvel eyed a bird perched on a dead stump. "What kind of bird is that?"

"That is a mockingbird. They make all sorts of sounds by mimicing other birds." With a loud cry the bird flew to the ground, ran a short distance, and then spread its gray wings to fly away.

As the day wore on, the air grew warmer. The boys shed their deerskin jackets and threw off the quilt. Pa slipped his hat under the seat and pointed to a grove of nearby trees. "Those are cottonwoods. There is a story that the Alamo got its name from that tree."

Marvel cocked his head to one side and declared, "Now, Pa, are you teasing us again?"

"Nope, not this time," his father laughed. "I understand there are a lot of cottonwoods in San Antonio. And those other trees are cypress. Back in Carolina where we came from, there are many tall trees that bloom in the spring. Sometimes I think your Ma gets homesick for Carolina. Maybe that is why she complains about the way we talk. She says that folks speak good English back there, but she is wrong. Most of them talk just like we do here. I remind her that the people of Texas have come from different places. Why, some are Europeans."

"What is a European?" Melton demanded.

"That means they are people from Europe," Marvel said.

"You are right, Marvel, and those folks came across the Atlantic Ocean to get here. Some came from Poland —the town of Panna Maria is a Polish town. New Braunfels was settled by the Germans."

Melton asked, "Why did folks come to Texas from Europe anyway?"

"That is a good question, boy. I reckon most of them wanted to start a new life in a new land. Maybe they wanted to be free. Freedom is mighty important. Folks should forget their differences in language and try to get along. Everybody should work together to make Texas a better place for the future."

Melton rested his blond head against the side of the wagon. There was a serious expression on his face when he said. "It is good to be free. Do you think that was why my folks were coming to Texas?"

"It could have been," Marvel nodded.

They rode along in silence, each thinking his own thoughts. Pa was pleased to see how serious his boys could be. He wanted them to learn about pride and freedom, and to have love for their fellowmen.

Melton's yell brought them back from their private dreams. "I'm hungry! Can't we eat?"

"I declare, boy, you are always hungry! But I reckon Cain and Abel could use a rest. Look, there is a stream up by those shade trees. We will stop there."

"Stream? Can we go wading?"

"Oh, can we, Pa? I don't know about you, Melton, but I'm hot."

"We will see," Pa replied. He tied the reins to a bush and, with the water bucket in his hand, headed for the water. The boys were right behind him. "It seems fresh enough," Pa said filling the bucket. "I reckon you can wade here near the bank after you finish eating."

It did not take them long to bite into Ma's corn bread and sausage. Rags appeared from nowhere to get his

14

share. Pa chuckled. "That dog is just like you, Melton. He is always hungry and ready to eat!"

The boys swallowed the last bite, wiped their hands on their pants, and slipped off their boots. Melton gave a shout and raced for the water, "Bet I beat you Marvel!" And he did. But, with the first splash, he discovered the water too cold for comfort and decided that throwing rocks was more fun than wading.

"Stay in sight, boys. Injuns might like this place, too."

A feeling of happiness filled Pa. He watched the boys and muttered softly. "This is the way life ought to be — free and happy." When he thought of Ma and the little ones back home, he felt ashamed to be so contented. He mumbled under his breath, "A fellow does what a fellow has to do."

With a yawn and sigh he reached for his map to study it carefully. Finally, satisfied that they were on the right trail, he returned it to his pocket, and lay back on the grass. Resting his arm under his head, he listened to the sounds: the oxen munching grass, the children's voices, and the soft swish of the leaves in the trees. Pa imagined he heard the grasses growing up from the rich earth. He smiled at the thought and decided he had daydreamed long enough.

"Boys, let's be on our way," he called, picking up his hat and gun. The sun was bright and warm. "Come on."

The two skidded a last rock over the water's surface and raced to the wagon. Once they were in their places, Pa scolded them. "You are all wet and muddy. Don't you sit on Ma's quilt, do you hear? We don't need it now, so I will put it in the back. And here's your dog. He is wet, too, and looks plumb tuckered out."

Pa was right. Rags's button nose was moist with sweat. His pink tongue hung to his chin. His fur was covered with mud.

"You are a mess, Rags," Marvel scolded. "Get down on the floor till you're dry, do you hear?" With his head hung low and his tail between his legs, the dog crawled under the seat."

"How could it be cold this morning and so hot now?" Melton moaned once they were on their way again.

"It's like that in Texas—winter one minute and summer the next. I reckon the sun causes it. Don't worry about putting your boots back on until your pants are dry."

Marvel's tone was serious. "Pa, we saw lots of tracks along the banks. Could they have been bear tracks?"

"Maybe. I understand they have found all sorts of animals in these parts."

"What kind of animals?"

"Oh, maybe wildcats, bears, coyotes, and panthers."

"Panthers?" Melton's eyes were round in wonder. "What's that?"

Pa stretched his arms apart as he said, "It's a big cat, maybe this big, that can run like the wind. I have never seen one, but I've heard they can run almost as fast as a horse!"

"Glory," Melton moaned. "I hope we don't meet one. Can they hurt you?"

"Almost any animal will hurt you if you are trying to catch them, Melton. A fellow can't be too careful. Remember that."

"I will. Say, how far have we come?"

His father glanced up at the sun. "It must be about noon. That means we have been on the road about six hours. According to our map, we must have passed Comfort some time ago."

"You sure are smart to make a map," Melton said admiringly.

"No, son," Pa laughed. "I just do what I have to do. Like when I tried my hand at farming. I planted beans and corn to keep us from starving. I learned in a hurry that I wasn't a farmer. Nosirree!"

With a yawn and a nod of his head, Marvel declared. "I'm no farmer either. I'm going to be a doctor, like I told you."

Pa teased the boy's curls and grinned. "Well, Doc, why don't you two crawl down there on the floor with Rags and take a nap? I will call you if I see anything unusual."

The boys were soon sound asleep beside their dog. The wagon continued up one hill and down another. Birds of various kinds and colors flitted through the trees, filling the air with their joyful song. Without the boys to keep him company, the afternoon passed slowly. Pa was half asleep when, suddenly, he saw two horsemen riding toward them. He reached for the gun he had put under the seat and nudged Marvel with his foot. "Boys. Wake up. There are a couple riders coming this way."

They scrambled to their places. Rags squeezed in between them to watch. One rider was tall and thin, the other was plump with a reddish-colored face. As their horses drew nearer, Pa called, "Howdy."

The men shouted back, "Howdy, strangers." They stopped beside the wagon and looked at Pa and the children.

The thin man removed his hat and wiped his face on his shirt sleeve. He said, "It sure is hot. Where are you going, mister?"

Pa studied their faces carefully and, deciding that they were friendly, relaxed his grip on his gun. "We are on our way to Goliad."

"Goliad?" the red-faced rider exclaimed in surprise. "Mister, you sure are brave! You had better hope you don't meet any Injuns."

The palms of Pa's hands grew clammy. A feeling of fear crept into his heart. "Injuns? Are there Injuns around here?"

The thin man chuckled as he answered Pa's question. "Who knows where they are? Or when they will strike."

"That is right. You never know they are around until it is too late," his partner agreed. "I heard they are up to their old tricks again — stealing horses and making trouble. They are sly."

Pa frowned. "What do you mean?"

"Well," the thin man drawled out his words slowly, "they are as still as mice."

"Sometimes quieter," the plump fellow mumbled. "Say, which way are you going to Goliad?"

"I understand that the best way is to go along the Guadalupe River to New Braunfels. From there we will follow the river to Gonzales. When we come to that town, we will cross the river and go on to Goliad. Do you think that is the safest way? Where do you fellows live?"

"We live on the other side of the river — north a few miles. I hate to tell you, mister, but the road back there is not real good. The ruts are mighty deep, you could have trouble. You might get stuck if you aren't careful. You might be smart to cross the river here. The water along here is fairly shallow. Once you are on the other side you just follow the road until you come to a bend in the river. You will see a mountain to the north. That is Devil's Backbone. You might make better time on the other side, that road is not traveled as much as this one."

"My brother Alonzo has told you right. Say, my name is Kirk — Ben Kirk. What is yours?"

"I am glad to meet you both. I am John Sellers, and these are my boys — Marvel and Melton. Kirk? Are you any kin to Joshua Kirk in Center Point?"

"He is our uncle. In fact, we are on our way to his place now. Say, I have heard my uncle talk of a doctor named Sellers. Do you happen to know him?" Ben asked.

Pa chuckled. "That's me. I reckon I don't look like a

18

doctor. My wife says I don't talk like one. I figure if somebody is sick they don't care how I talk."

The brothers laughed. Alonzo said, "I want a doctor I can understand, that's for sure." Glancing toward the setting sun, he sighed. "Sorry we can't sit and talk longer, Doc. But Uncle Joshua is expecting us before midnight, so we had better be on our way."

With those words, the two men spurred their horses and rode away. Ben called back over his shoulder. *"Vaya usted con Dios, amigos!"*

The boys watched until they vanished from view. Marvel asked. "What did he say. Pa?"

"He was speaking Spanish. He said 'Go with God, friends!' " Pa scratched his head and stared at the road ahead of him. "That road does look pretty rough. Shall we take their advice and cross over?"

"Whatever you think, Pa," Marvel said.

Pa directed the oxen off onto the weeds and headed for the river bank. He paused long enough to let the animals drink. "That Kirk fellow was right — the water is shallow. Giddy-up, Cain and Abel, we will be making camp over there."

Once they were on the opposite side, Pa looked at the boys. "Say, you have been mighty quiet, Melton. Has the cat got your tongue?"

Melton shook his head. "Nope, I've been thinking."

"About what?" Marvel demanded.

"I was thinking about why Pa kept his gun in his hands while he talked to those men. Did you think they might cause trouble, Pa?"

Pa had not realized the boy had noticed the gun. "We can't be too careful, son. There are a lot of good people in the world, but Texas has its share of bad ones, too. We must be careful. Of course, I would not think of shooting unless I had to. A doctor tries to save lives, not take them. But folks are always saying 'Don't judge a book by its cover.' That means that things are not always the way they look."

"What do you mean?"

"Well, Melton, I recall the prettiest snake I ever saw was red and yellow and black. But—that snake could kill a fellow! Your Ma is always telling the girls, 'Pretty is as pretty does.' Just because a thing looks pretty does not mean it is good. Remember that."

4

The Rattlesnake

"It's clouding up," Pa said, glancing up at the sky. "I reckon this is as good a place as any to stop. We will make camp over yonder near those trees. While I'm watering and hobbling the team, you look for wood."

The wagon rolled to a stop beneath the grove of moss-laden oaks. Rags wasted no time. Once he was on the ground he vanished quickly among the high weeds, leaving the boys to search for wood. They found plenty of branches and limbs nearby. In the meantime, Pa unhitched the wooden yoke and walked the oxen toward the river to water them. When he returned, he tied the oxen's back legs together with a short rope so that they could not wander too far away from camp.

"Boys, I will help carry the wood. Where are you?"

"Over here."

Pa picked up his gun and headed in their direction. As he rounded a clump of bushes, he walked into a cleared area and saw the boys. Melton was bending down to pick up a large stick. Marvel, carrying an armload of wood, was approaching a large rock. Suddenly, Marvel gave a bloodcurdling scream and dropped the wood. Then Pa saw it—a rattlesnake! It lay coiled on the rock with its tail making a whirring noise.

Marvel froze. As Pa raised his gun, he saw the brown and black diamond markings on the snake! He knew his aim meant life or death for his son. His bullet might miss and hit the child, or the snake could strike in that split second. But he had no choice! Never in all of his life had Pa held the life of his own child in his hands. He refused to think of that as he pulled the trigger. The noise was deafening. He closed his eyes and muttered a prayer as he dropped his gun to his side.

It took courage for Pa to open his eyes. What he saw made him weak. Marvel lay in a heap on the ground. The loathsome creature's head was inches from his hand. Its body lay twisting and wriggling nearby. Pa's years of medical training took over as he knelt beside the still child. His experienced hands went to work. After a quick examination, Pa heaved a sigh of relief. Marvel had collapsed from fear and shock. He was not hurt.

"You are all right, son. And the snake is dead. See?"

Marvel's lashes fluttered.

Pa went on. "You just had a scare — we all did. Let's get up now and take this wood back to camp and make a fire. You will feel better then."

Behind them, Melton had been rooted where he stood. He had watched the gruesome scene, too weak and terrified to move. Now he saw Marvel struggle to his feet, staring at the snake's beady eyes as he slowly backed away.

"Glory, Pa, Marvel is sure lucky you can shoot! What a close call! Say, let's get away from this place — it gives me the shivers!"

Pa wasted no time in building a fire and seeing that the children ate a good meal of Ma's ham and baked potatoes. Rags suddenly appeared for his share, much to Pa's disgust. "Some dog you are! Off chasing rabbits when you are needed, but always ready for a handout. Marvel, do you feel all right? You haven't said much."

"I have been thinking. If you hadn't blown its head off, that snake would have killed me. You saved my life."Suddenly, the outline of a dead tree caught his eye. The leafless branches seemed to twist like hundreds of wiggling snakes. The boy shuddered at the thought.

"Well, look here at what your Ma sent for a surprise," Pa said, handing each of the boys a fried blackberry tart. "While you are eating that, I will go back and get those rattles. Then you will know that critter is really dead, son, and you can stop worrying about it."

A short time later he returned, holding Marvel's trophy. "That was some snake! Why, it must have been five feet long and it had nine rattles. See? We will leave them here by the fire overnight so they can dry out. You know, boys, I was thinking about the old wive's tale that a snake won't crawl over a rope. It won't hurt any to lay our rope around the wagon. You might sleep better just knowing it is there. But first, I'd better lower the canvas that's behind the seat. It might rain during the night."

Pa crawled up to unfasten the rope that held the front cover in place. When the canvas started down, a shiny harmonica — which had been hidden in the folds — fell to the floor. "Look what I found! It's the mouth organ you lost, Marvel! Now, I wonder how it got in there?"

"There is no telling," Marvel declared happily, putting it to his lips to play. He began to blow. Rags cocked his shaggy head to one side and howled at the squeaky noises filling the air.

Pa roared with laughter. "Boy, that dog is saying we have had enough excitement for one day. He is right. It's bedtime. Now go get into the wagon while I add more wood to the fire."

Rags sat underneath the wagon, listening to them settle down for the night. Once everything was still, he started howling again.

"Oh, Pa," Marvel cried. "Poor Rags wants up here,

too. He's afraid to sleep down there all alone. Besides, he doesn't want to get wet if it rains."

His father chuckled and pulled the dog up beside them. "We had better hope your Ma will understand when she hears he slept on her good quilt."

The boys giggled at the thought and placed the dog between them. Suddenly, the stillness was broken by a sound that sent chills up their spines.

Marvel whispered hoarsely, "What is that?"

"Just a coyote calling to his friends. Don't worry, they are far away. We are safe."

The boys were soon sound asleep. Pa Sellers lay thinking about their first day and the snake. He thought of the miles ahead and the warning about the Indians. He wondered if he had made a mistake heading for Goliad with the boys.

5

Remembering the Alamo

When Marvel opened his eyes the next morning, he wondered where he was. Then he heard his father. "Come on, sleepy heads. It is time to get up. Hurry! Breakfast is about ready. Get dressed, boys, and go wash your faces."

It did not take them long to put on their boots and, coats in hand, head for the river. Rags was right behind when they raced back to the campfire.

"That bacon sure smells good. I'm starving."

"You are always hungry," Marvel teased. "You and Rags. Look at him."

The dog's eyes were fixed on the corn cakes and bacon that Pa was dishing up. "I figured I would cook plenty so we would have some left to go with our beans. We are about out of Ma's cooking. We will have to be on the lookout for something — fried rabbit might taste good." While he talked, Pa filled their cups with coffee and the last of the milk. Placing Rags's portion on the ground, he announced. "Let's eat." The dog had not waited for those words. His dish was already empty.

It looks like it is going to be a pretty day," Pa said brushing the crumbs from his chin. "You boys can take the dishes down to the river and wash them while I hitch up the oxen. I reckon I had better put out this fire or else the sparks could blow and catch the brush on fire. We don't want that." He kicked dirt upon the hot coals while he talked. Cold chills raced up Pa's back when the toe of his shoe touched the rattles of Marvel's snake. "Do you want those, son?" When Marvel picked them up and put them in his pocket, Pa promised himself that he would be more watchful from now on.

The boys tossed the dishes into the back of the wagon after they were washed and then crawled up on the wagon seat. "Here is your dog," Pa said, getting beside them. "Giddy-up, Cain and Abel. Let's go."

Rags snuggled under the quilt between the boys and went to sleep. "We are getting a late start this morning, but it's still pretty chilly. I reckon we are about fifteen miles from home. If we are lucky we will get to the bend in the river before dark. What was it that Kirk fellow called that mountain? It had a name. But I can't recall what it was."

With a thoughtful expression on his face, Marvel scratched his head. "It seems like it was Devil's something. But what?"

"Devil's Backbone," Melton answered proudly.

"That's right—Devil's Backbone!" Pa chuckled softly. He never minded their questions or telling them stories, for they were always learning. He often thought their young minds were like limestone absorbing water, the way they absorbed things in their heads.

"Look at that silly bird with its tail stuck in the air running in front of Abel," Marvel said.

"That is a roadrunner or chaparral. Funny thing, that mother bird lays maybe three or more white eggs days apart so they hatch at different times. That way the new babies keep the unhatched eggs warm while the mamma and papa birds look for food."

Melton cocked his head to one side, mimicking the strange looking bird. "What do they eat? Worms?"

"No snakes! Sometimes they eat lizards too long for their mouths. The bird gulps down the head, but the lizard's tail hangs out!"

"Ugh, lizards! That doesn't make me hungry!" Melton groaned in disgust.

"I am glad to hear that," Pa laughed. "Another thing that is interesting, I heard the roadrunner will kill a snake that tries to get her chicks. But protecting the little ones is natural to most creatures."

"You protected me or I wouldn't be here. Pa." Marvel shivered at the thought. "Let's don't talk about that. Say, would you tell us about the Alamo? You said we would go to San Antonio on the way home."

His father relaxed the reins and shifted to a more comfortable position to start his story. "Well, you know we weren't here in 1836, but Texas was part of Mexico then. The folks that did live here weren't happy about some of the new laws the Mexican government passed. I reckon they liked the idea of being free. They picked Stephen F. Austin as their leader and, when he was sent to Washington, General Sam Houston took his place. When it looked like there was going to be trouble with Mexico, Houston sent James Bowie to San Antonio with orders to blow up the Alamo."

"Blow it up?"

"Why would they want to do that?" Marvel demanded.

"It seems that Houston felt the Alamo wasn't worth holding, but he didn't want the Mexicans to have it. Since Colonel William Travis was in charge of the Alamo, he and Bowie decided to take a stand against the Mexican army."

"And Santa Anna was the general of that army, wasn't he?"

"You're right, Marvel." Pa cleared his throat and went on with his story. "Colonel Travis stationed a lookout in the church tower. When the sentinel spotted Santa Anna's army of over 5,000 men, Travis ordered his group to fall back inside the walls of the Alamo. And, on February twenty-third, the fighting started. The cannons boomed for thirteen days and nights."

27

Marvel spoke up. "Why didn't Travis send for help?"

"He did, son. First, he sent a letter addressed to 'The people of Texas and all Americans in the world.' He also wrote 'I shall never surrender or retreat.' "

"Didn't anybody go to help? I would have gone," Melton vowed.

"Me, too. Wasn't Davy Crockett there?"

"Thirty-two men from Gonzales went. Crockett and his boys from Tennessee were there, too. You know, folks tell stories about Crockett. I reckon some are true and some aren't. He was supposed to have said 'Be sure you're right; then go ahead.' He must have thought it right to fight and die for freedom because that is what he did. Him and about 180 others died there at the Alamo."

"What day was that, Pa?"

"Melton, that was a day Texas will never forget — March 6, 1836. Those brave men in the Alamo fought hard, but old Santa Anna had them outnumbered from the start. Just remember, those Texans went down fighting for what they thought was right." Pa's voice showed his feelings. He always got a lump in his throat when he thought of Travis and his men. "Well, with the battle cry 'Remember the Alamo,' General Houston's army met the Mexicans at San Jacinto. The Texans defeated Santa Anna's men at the Battle of San Jacinto in twenty minutes on April 21."

"Hurrah for Houston!" Melton shouted, waving his hat in the air.

"Hurrah for Texas!" With that shout, Marvel pulled the harmonica from his pocket to fill the morning with his music.

"Why don't we sing that song you said the Texans sang when they marched against Santa Anna?"

Pa rumpled Melton's blond curls playfully and began to sing. Their voices, along with the wailing harmonica and howling dog, filled the peaceful valley as the day wore on.

6

Turkey Chase

"I hope you don't think I'm bragging, but I think I'm getting pretty good playing this harmonica," Marvel said sheepishly. "Someday I would sure like to have a fiddle. You know there is something about music that makes me feel good all over. Does that sound funny?"

Pa shook his head. "I can understand that, son. Music helps a fellow forget his cares and woes. It makes me want to tap my toes."

The boys agreed and settled back to enjoy the ride. The first day's excitement had vanished. The morning grew warmer. Mile after mile the squeaky wagon traveled up one hill and down another. The boys took turns yawning in their struggle to keep awake. Pa, too, was having trouble keeping his eyes open. But any thought of sleep was forgotten after the wagon began to wobble and sway over the deep holes in the trail.

"Easy there, Cain and Abel," Pa scolded.

"We would likely be in Goliad if we had brought the horses."

"Maybe, Melton, but I figured it was best not to tempt the Injuns into stealing them. Say, did I ever tell you about the things folks brought to this land from Europe?"

"What kind of things?" Marvel asked.

"Oh, things like guns, iron, steel, and horses. Did you know there were none of them here until the Spaniards brought them?"

"No horses?"

Marvel's brows went up in surprise. "You mean the Injuns didn't have horses before then?"

"That's right, they had never even seen a horse! The Injuns had always hunted deer, buffalo, and other animals on foot. When the Injuns saw how fast the horses could travel, they wanted them, too. The Comanches learned how to make saddles and horsehide bridles by watching the Spaniards. They also learned to slip a loop around a horseneck to hang over the animal's side to get away from bullets and arrows. When the Spanish brought more and more horses, they let some run wild. And it didn't take the Injuns long to claim them for their own. The Injuns also learned how to steal horses. I reckon most of them — especially the Comanches — just took to riding."

Melton asked, "Even the children?"

His father nodded his head. "Yep! I've heard that they can ride by the time they can walk. Comanches believe the greatest thing a boy, or brave, can do is to be a warrior. Their bravest fighter is the war chief, and his shield means three things: brave hunter, mighty warrior, and a good rider. Most young braves dream of being a chief. Death holds no fear for them. I understand the Comanches think there is life after death in a place beyond the setting sun. That is like a happy hunting ground in the sky."

The children watched the road, absent-mindedly thinking about their father's words. Melton pictured Pa's two black horses back in Center Point as he watched the oxen. "So that is why we brought Cain and Abel? The Injuns might have tried to steal your horses, right? What kind do they like anyway?"

Pa laughed. "Almost any kind they can get, but spotted pintos seem to be their favorite. A pure white horse is the prettiest, but there aren't many of those. I guess that is why most Injuns worship a white horse or buffalo."

Marvel stared at Melton's hair and grinned. "Say, you are almost white-headed. I wonder if the Injuns would worship you?"

"I'm not a horse!"

"Sometimes you are hungry as a horse," Marvel teased.

"Now what did you say that for? You just reminded me — I'm hungry!"

"I figured it was about that time."

"Cain and Abel could use a rest, so we will stop. There is plenty of grass around here without me unhitching them. You two can get the oxen some water, and I will get things ready. We can eat under that shade tree over yonder."

Once the wagon came to a stop, the boys hit the ground. Pa and the dog were not far behind. While the boys took the bucket to the nearby stream to get the water for the oxen, Pa brought the food from the wagon. He caught an occasional glimpse of the dog's black tail tagging after the children when they raced toward the tree. They wasted no time on words but listened to the sounds of nature while they ate the last of their sausage and corn bread.

When Melton finished he licked his fingers muttering, "I wish Ma was here."

"I know you, boy," his father chuckled. "You are just thinking about her cooking. And if we don't find something by suppertime we will all be thinking about her. Bacon and corn meal is all that's left."

"Bacon? Bacon is for breakfast," Melton moaned. "I would like something sweet."

"Say, I just remembered — Ma sent us some agarita jelly! That would taste mighty good with the rest of this

31

corn bread." The boys quickly agreed. Pa soon returned from the wagon with a jar of jelly. They watched with interest as he coated the bread with a thick layer of it. The boys gobbled it down like two hungry animals and wished for more.

With a sigh of contentment Pa leaned against the tree and said, "I never will forget our first agarita jelly. When someone told Ma the berries made good eating, she picked some and put them in a bucket. It wasn't long until her hands and arms were burning something awful. Since I wasn't sure what was wrong, I gave her a dose of my Mama's special herb formula. It eased the itching and she went to sleep. I spread herb salve on her poor red hands and arms. Later, we learned she should have shook the berries off onto a cloth and should not have touched the bush. That's a lesson she will never forget. Nosirree!"

"Tell us more."

"Well, we learned about the different plants and trees here. Some are good, some bad. We had lots to learn when we first came to Texas."

"What is in your special medicine that made Ma go to sleep?" Marvel asked. "I might need to know that when I get to be a doctor."

His father rubbed his whiskers thoughtfully. "Lots of plants. One is a passion flower—they grow around these parts. I understand the Injuns even use the passion flower for medicine. But, boys, don't you eat anything unless you're sure it is safe. Lots of plants and leaves look harmless, but they can kill a fellow."

"Like those?" Melton pointed to a patch of umbrella-like caps not far from them. "Toadstools can kill you if you eat them."

"Sure, everybody knows that."

"Shh," Melton whispered. "What's that?"

"What's what?" his father demanded.

Suddenly alert and tense, the three listened in silence. Then Pa heard it—the faint "cackle-cackle" sound.

He relaxed and chuckled. "Son, you just heard your supper! Those are turkeys! Keep the dog here while I see if I can shoot one."

Gun in hand, he paused and listened. "Sounds like they are over that way." He pointed to the green wall of trees in front of them. "I will go around and try to come in above them. If they head this way you try to chase them toward the river. Maybe we can corner one there. But remember, when I yell 'stop,' you stop. I might hit one of you instead of a turkey! You had better put this rope on Rags to keep him here with you. I don't need him."

Pa tossed them the rope used to hobble the oxen. He mumbled to himself, "Turkeys, here I come."

Rags scarcely moved when the rope was slipped over his head. Marvel explained softly, "Be still now. You want something to eat besides bacon, don't you?"

With his ears lifted high, the dog cocked his head to one side to study the boys. He knew something was about to happen, but he was not sure what it was. Neither were the boys.

"Listen," Melton spoke in a low whisper. "I think Pa found them."

The three, tense with excitement, strained to listen. A chorus of deep gobbling sounds gradually turned to high-pitched squawks. Then — silence. They waited breathlessly. Where was Pa?

The dog pulled at the end of the rope, staring intently at the bushes right in front of them. The leaves rustled noisily as a wild-eyed, half-grown turkey tom sprang into the clearing. Pa was not far behind with his arms flapping.

The children gave a whoop to join the chase. Marvel darted past his father in hot pursuit of the turkey. The terrified bird complained bitterly and extended his wings for flight. In the confusion Melton tripped over the dog, who had broken the rope and was frantically darting this

33

way and that to catch the creature. The tom escaped their clutches by leaping to an overhead limb. Pa did not wait; he aimed and fired. The turkey screeched in pain when his tail feathers left his body. Then seeing his chance, he soared over their heads to hit the ground on the run. Marvel and his dog were hot on his trail. Pa struggled to stay in the race but, with his shirttail flapping and his beard full of feathers, his heart was not in it. He paused to reload his gun and catch his breath. At that moment, without warning, the turkey decided to double back. Pa yelled, "Stop!"

The peaceful silence was shattered as he pulled the trigger and prepared to reload. The bird wobbled strangely and slowly collapsed at the edge of the river.

The children clapped their hands cheering, "You got him, Pa! See? Rags knows he's dead!" The dog sniffed the lifeless form and wagged his tail.

"He's dead all right," Pa agreed as he picked up the bird. "Poor critter never knew what hit him."

"What will we do now?"

With the turkey in one hand and his gun in the other, his father turned toward the wagon. "We will tie him up, Melton, and clean him later. We had better get moving and then make camp early."

Marvel stared at his father and giggled. "Pa, you look like a turkey too. You have got more feathers than that bird! They are all over you!" The boys laughed so hard the tears rolled down their cheeks but, for some reason, Pa did not find anything to laugh about.

He groaned, shook his head and brushed his clothes. "Mercy, I'm plumb tuckered out! Marvel run and get the bucket while I tie up this critter on the wagon."

Melton watched him tie the tom to the side of the wagon. "Glory, what a way to get our supper! Can we do it again?"

His father gave him a tired look and moaned wearily. "Sakes no, boy! Don't you even think of such a thing.

I haven't enough strength to ever do that again." The children laughed in spite of themselves.

When they were on their way once more, Marvel said, "I only wish we could play in the water. But I reckon that turkey chase was more fun. If we stop early, can we go exploring?" Pa nodded half-heartedly. He had no desire to go exploring anywhere.

Melton rested his chin in his hands thoughtfully. "I want to know something. Where did the other turkeys go? We heard a bunch of them, but I only saw one."

His father cast a surprised look in his direction and replied, "I was wondering the same thing. They must have a roost across the river in those high rocks over there." He pointed to the opposite bank. "There could be a cave or crevice in those cliffs. I understand there are lots of caves around these parts. Maybe they found a hiding place."

Marvel unraveled a loose end of the rope that lay at his feet and took the snake's rattle from his pocket. "Do you think I could hang this around my neck like a lucky charm?"

"I don't see why not, boy."

"I will tie it," Melton said. "Pa, you sure are brave."

"No, Melton. Pa did what a fellow has to do. He was protecting his youngun because he loved me."

His father hid his smile with his hand. He realized his son was merely repeating his own words. "That's right, Marvel, I did what I had to do. I would do it for any of you. I love all five of my younguns."

"You would fight for us if you had to, Pa."

His father smiled. "That's right, Melton, I sure would. Fighting just to fight isn't the thing a fellow ought to do. It won't prove a thing. But fighting to protect yourself— or what is yours—that is the only thing a fellow can do."

John Sellers never dreamed he would have to prove his words very soon.

7

A
Lesson

They spent the rest of the afternoon laughing about the turkey hunt. Melton's mouth watered as he thought about how delicious it would taste. "Oh, I just can't wait to get a bite of that turkey."

"I am not sure it will taste so good. It could be tough like cow's hide since we are cooking it over the campfire. Let's hope it isn't half raw like Injun meat. Of course, Injuns don't eat turkey."

"They don't eat turkey? Why not? It tastes mighty good to me." With a devilish twinkle in his eyes, Marvel added, "Well, it tastes good when Ma cooks in anyway."

Pa scratched his beard thoughtfully. "To tell the truth, I don't know why Injuns won't eat birds. I reckon it is that their customs are just different from ours."

"Different? How?"

"Oh, in lots of ways. For one thing, the women do most of the work."

"Ma does most of the work around our place. Of course, you are always away doctoring sick folks." His father had to agree with Melton there.

"You told us that their tepees were folded when they traveled. Who puts them up again? How long does it take anyway?"

"The squaws—that's their word for women—can put one up in less than fifteen minutes and take it down in about five!"

"That is fast! What else is so different about Injuns?"

His father rubbed his chin, thinking about how to answer Melton's question. "Well, some Injuns have more than one wife." He waited for their reply.

"Pa," Melton scolded, "You're teasing us again. More than one wife? What for? You have only Ma, isn't one enough?"

With a chuckle, Pa agreed. "You are right there, son. Ma's enough for me. I reckon Injuns figure that since the squaws do most of the work anyway, the more wives they have the more work will be done. One wife bosses the others."

"Ma wouldn't like that!"his son declared firmly.

"That's like having slaves, isn't it?"

Pa looked at the ten-year-old in surprise. "Melton, I do believe you are the thinkingest youngun I ever saw."

"What about me?" Marvel demanded jealously. "Aren't I a thinker?"

"Boy, you are a fighter—like the Texas Rangers. You are for action, always willing to jump right in the middle of things. But that's good. It takes both kinds— the doers and the thinkers."

"What is a Texas Ranger?"

Pa cleared his throat and moved to a more comfortable position to begin his tale. "You understand, now, that what I am telling happened before we got here, way back when Texas was still part of Mexico. I have told you about folks coming here to settle. They traveled mostly in groups, located their land, and started a home. They put up cabins in a hurry—planning to build better ones later on."

"Didn't the cabins leak when it rained?"

"They sure did, Marvel! I didn't know which was worse—the wind and cold of the winter or the bugs and

37

heat of the summer. Folks tried to keep out the cold by packing mud between the logs. A good rain could wash it right out. There were other troubles, too."

"Like what?"

"Injuns! They didn't take too kindly to folks settling on their hunting land."

"But Pa," Melton reasoned, "who was there first? Wasn't it the Injun?"

Pa squinted one eye to stare at the boy. "Whose side are you on anyway? Sure, Injuns were there first, but the settlers had government papers saying the land was theirs. Folks never knew when the Injuns would go on the warpath. So, in about 1835, the Texas Rangers were formed to protect the settlements. Last year — in 1859 — President Sam Houston added more Rangers to keep the peace."

"Can the Rangers really fight?" Marvel asked.

"You bet they can, and the Injuns know it!" With an upward glance at the sky, Pa said, "I reckon we had better make camp if we are going to cook that turkey. This looks like a good spot. We won't have far to go for water with the river just over there. First, we will need to build a fire and boil some water so that we can get this bird ready to cook. Whoa, Cain and Abel, we are stopping for the night."

The boys and their dog were on the ground before the wheels stopped rolling. Rags shook himself, sniffed the air, and headed for the weeds.

It was not long before Pa had a roaring fire going in the clearing near the wagon. They carried water from the river and put it on to heat. Pa brought the turkey from the wagon. "Would you like to pull some feathers?"

"Sure," Melton said, reaching for a fistful. But he and Marvel quickly discovered they could not pull the feathers. They would not budge. "How are we going to get them off? We can't eat feathers, can we?"

"If the water is hot enough I will show you." Pa decided it was. He grasped the bird with one hand and poured the hot water over the turkey with the other hand. Then he said, "Now pull."

The feathers now came out easily. Feathers were soon flying everywhere. Some landed on the sizzling coals. As they burned they gave off an unpleasant odor.

Melton groaned, "Glory! Doesn't that stink? What a smell!"

Rags lifted his head and quickly retreated into the weeds after taking one sniff.

8

The Accident

The next morning while Pa cooked breakfast, Marvel's head appeared around the side of the wagon. "Morning, Pa. That bacon smells mighty good." He jumped to the ground and headed toward the river yelling back over his shoulder, "You are a slowpoke, Melton. I will beat you if you don't hurry up."

Melton raced in that direction, but he was too late. Marvel was already there. The delicate fragrances of coffee and burning wood mingled with the sizzling bacon. "You won't beat me going back." Melton yelled, coming to a halt beside his father. "Is breakfast ready? I'm hungry!"

"How could you be? Last night you ate half that turkey. Didn't he, Rags?" The playful dog wagged his tail barking excitedly.

"I will get you for that, Rags," Melton laughed, running at the dog. Seeing his chance for a game of tag, Rags darted off with Melton at his heels. The two chased first one way and then the other, drawing nearer and nearer to the fire.

"Careful there," Pa warned, but he was too late. There was no way he could have prevented the accident that followed. The toe of Melton's boot hit one of the burning logs, causing it to roll into the dog's path. Rags tried in vain to stop, but he could not. Marvel watched his pet's paws meet the glowing wood! A spine-tingling howl went up from the animal. He sank to the ground in pain.

Marvel was immediately on his knees beside the injured dog. "Oh, Pa, he has burned his feet something awful."

The doctor ran to the water barrel to wet the gunny sack he had used as a pot holder. He hurried back with it and squatted on the ground beside his son to examine the dog.

"He got burned all right," Dr. Sellers declared, wrapping the paws with the wet sack while he talked. "Hand me that slab of bacon and the knife, Marvel, then hold this on here while I cut a slice of bacon. This water will ease the pain for the moment till I can wrap the burns with bacon. The fat in the meat will help pull out the soreness and help the blisters. I reckon he needs a dab of my special herb medicine to make him sleep."

"While I'm doing this, son, go and fix a place for him under the wagon seat. Holler when you are ready and I will carry him over. Poor critter is going to be sore and tender for a few days. We don't want dirt getting in the blisters while he is healing." All the time he talked Pa was carefully wrapping the dog's paws. Rags seemed to understand Pa was trying to help him. "Don't worry, everything is all right. You will feel better after you have slept a spell. It won't hurt so bad. But I figure I had better tie this bacon on here so it will stay in place. We don't want you eating it when you wake up, and knowing you, that is about what you would do."

Marvel tried to smile at his father's joke, but it was not easy. "I'm ready, Pa," he called after spreading his coat under the wagon seat. Pa lifted the whining animal in his arms. Rags's pitiful cries tore at Pa's heart as he carried him to the wagon and placed him on the coat. Marvel stretched out beside him. "Don't cry, Rags," he whispered. "Pa says you will be all right. He is going to give you something to make you sleep. You will feel better when you wake up. "Pa said you would."

The tip of the dog's black tail moved ever so slightly. The injured dog tried to lick Marvel's tear-streaked cheek, but he was in too much pain.

Swallowing the lump in his throat, Pa muttered softly, "Son, move over so I can give him this medicine. It won't hurt him. It will help him go to sleep." The dog's sorrowful eyes watched Pa hide the medicine in a small chunk of turkey. "Here, Rags, take this. It will ease the pain." Rags opened his mouth obediently and swallowed the meat.

Marvel and his father watched in silence as the pathetic groans grew softer. Gradually, Rags's tense body went limp. His eyes closed. The dog lay deathly still.

"Pa, are you sure he will be all right? He will wake up, won't he?" Marvel's chin trembled as he stared at his father with tear-filled eyes. "He won't die, will he?"

Pa's strong arms went around his son. Whispering a silent prayer, he nodded slowly. "Trust me, son. I want what is best for you. That goes for your dog, too. You children are dearer to me than life itself — I would put your health and happiness above my own." Tears rimmed Pa's eyes, too. He wiped them on his sleeve. "Now aren't we a pair, crying like this? Say, where is Melton? You don't suppose he has starved to death, do you? We had better check on him."

They found Melton huddled against the wheel of the wagon with his head buried in his knees. He was crying uncontrollably. Pa bent down and took him in his arms.

Melton buried his face against his father's chest, sobbing, "Oh, Pa. It was all my fault."

"No, son. It was not your fault. You didn't mean for Rags to get hurt." He clasped the boy tightly while he tried to comfort him. "Accidents do happen."

"But, Pa, I should have known better."

"That could have happened to anybody," Marvel soothed, "even to Pa or me. Isn't that right, Pa? Besides, Pa says Rags will be all right, so stop crying."

Suddenly, Pa sniffed and stiffened. The air was filled with the smell of burning bacon. He raced for the fire, but he was too late. The meat was burned black!

With a half-hearted grin, Pa declared, "I reckon breakfast could not wait for us. We will have to eat some of last night's turkey with this corn pone. I just hope the coffee is all right. I need a cup. I will add some water or else it will be strong enough to walk!"

Marvel's thoughts were on his dog as he watched Pa cut the turkey. "That will taste good. I will save some of mine. I know Rags will be hungry when he wakes up."

Melton's face brightened. Drying his tears with the back of his hand, he said, "And I will save some corn bread. Rags will like that."

"We should be glad this was already cooked," Pa muttered, filling their plates with corn bread and turkey. "You stay here. I will get some water from the barrel and take a look at Rags." He returned with a smile to report, "He is sleeping like a baby."

With a sigh of relief they ate in silence. Each was thinking how quickly things could change: first the snake, then the turkey, now their dog—all in a twinkling of an eye, without any warning. What would happen next?

Pa pushed the hair out of his face and said, "We are getting a mighty late start, but it can't be helped. While I'm hitching up Cain and Abel you boys wash the dishes and this coffee pot. You had better take Ma's lye soap along. This pot's burned black. Maybe if you rub it on the rocks it will cut some of the soot that is on the bottom."

"All right, Pa, but could I just take a peek at Rags?"

"We will both have a look at our patient."

They crept silently into the wagon and sat down beside the dog. His breathing seemed peaceful and relaxed. Marvel stroked Rags gently while his father checked the bandages.

Pa smiled, whispering softly, "See? He's going to be fine. Now let's get busy."

Melton's downcast expression caught Marvel's eye when he reached for the coffee pot. "Cheer up. Pa says Rags will be fine. He's sleeping like a log. Now, get those dishes and come on — there is work to do. I will race you to the river." They started off with the metal dishes clanging noisily.

Pa took the reins from the wagon seat and reached for his gun, but somehow Marvel had buried it under the coat that Rags was lying on. Pa decided he would not need a gun just to hitch the oxen. Besides, he thought with a grin, no need disturbing the patient. Rope in hand, he turned to find the oxen. He finally located them in the tall weeds some distance from camp. He wondered how they had wandered so far away.

"Whoa, stand still," he muttered to the animals as he bent down to untie their legs. Little did Pa realize what was about to happen.

Down at the river's edge, Melton was watching the dishes sink into the shallow water. Marvel was crouched beside the bank with the coffee pot. The tiny minnows that had been swimming lazily by the bank quickly darted to safety as he rubbed the bottom of the pot back and forth over the loose pebbles.

Melton's thoughts were on the dog while he washed the dishes. "I wonder how long Rags will sleep?"

"I don't know. Pa said he might sleep a while — whatever that means." Marvel emptied the pot and looked at the bottom. "It's still black," he grumbled unhappily. "This soap better —"

Suddenly, someone clamped a hand over Marvel's mouth and pinned his arms to his sides. He was too surprised to move. Then he glanced in Melton's direction. The younger boy was struggling and fighting to get free from an Indian. Marvel knew he had to do something, but what? He felt himself being pulled upon the grassy bank. He kicked his legs in protest, but his efforts were useless. A second Indian gagged his mouth and tied Marvel's wrists together. The first Indian leaped upon a pony to wait for the second one to toss Marvel up in front of him. Marvel's heart sank as they galloped off toward the trees.

When Melton realized he was left alone, he wiggled and twisted like a snake in an effort to break the Indian's grasp. He kicked first one way and then another. When his captor gave a moan, Melton kicked him again. The Indian muttered an oath under his breath and half-carried, half-dragged Melton's squirming body to another pony. Before Melton knew what was happening, he was gagged and tied. He kicked and bucked like a wild animal. Suddenly, Melton felt a sharp pain on his head. Everything went black. Melton did not know until much later that his movements had alerted Pa.

In the meantime, Pa was unhobbling the oxen when he heard a strange sound. He stood up and listened. At first he thought he must have been mistaken, then he heard it again — scuffling noises were coming from the direction of the river. Pa dropped the reins and raced through the weeds to the wagon. He grabbed his gun and ran frantically toward the river. He was too late. The boys were gone. When he caught a glimpse of the Indian ponies galloping toward the grove of trees, chills raced up his spine.

"Melton," he gasped, catching sight of the boy's white head leaning against the Indian. Then he saw Marvel! A feeling of helplessness swept over him as he watched the four ponies join the Indian party.

They were too far away for Pa to shoot, but he fired anyway. He fired again before they vanished behind the trees at the base of the mountain. The name Devil's

Backbone flashed in his mind. "This is hell to me," he groaned.

But what could he do? The gun sank to his side. His shoulders slumped. His eyes fell on the blackened pot at his feet. Moccasin tracks in the soft dirt and signs of a scuffle told him the boys had struggled to resist their attackers. Pa could almost picture what had happened. The boys had been so busy talking about Rags that they had not heard the Indians creeping up behind them until it was too late.

Pa shook his head and, grabbing the pot, gave a yell. He threw the coffee pot at the footprints. Cool water splashed up into his face, bringing him to his senses. He grabbed the pot and dishes and with the gun under one arm, raced for the wagon. He tossed them inside and gathered the things from around the fire. His hands were shaking with anger while he hitched the wagon.

"Giddy-up, hurry, hurry!" While he talked, Pa was remembering tales of Indians torturing and killing their captives. "Only one thing I can do," he mumbled under his breath, "get help to go look for them."

Pa knew he had to find a horse somewhere—fast.

9

Kidnapped!

Marvel and his Indian captor rode swiftly toward the trees to join the band of Indians. The brave held Marvel tightly in front of him with one arm and guided the horse with the other. In all of his eleven years the boy had never felt so helplessly alone. Then suddenly, his heart beat wildly with excitement as he heard the shots from back near the river.

"That was Pa's gun!" Marvel thought to himself. "He saw these Injuns. He will find a way to get us back."

Melton did not hear the shots as he sped along with his kidnapper. He was unconscious. The ponies avoided the cacti and other thorny plants as they raced over the rocky ground. Melton groaned and opened his eyes. It took him a while to understand what was happening. Once the boy realized where he was, he struggled to escape. The Indian hit him again. Melton went limp. The hair around the gash on his head turned red. Blood trickled down Melton's cheek.

Up and down the rolling ridges the Indians rode in a northwesterly direction. The hot sun beat on their heads. When they came to a river, Marvel was sure it was not the Guadalupe they had crossed in the wagon. The ponies slowly picked their way down the steep bank and into the deep water to swim toward the opposite bank. The water crept up Marvel's legs and thighs. He shivered from the cold and looked for Melton. Marvel hoped the boy would not be foolish enough to try to escape in the river; he could not swim. Marvel knew there was a time to be daring, but this was not the time.

He finally spotted Melton when the ponies were making their way up on the other side of the river. Melton's face was bloody. Between tears of anger and frustration, Marvel realized for the first time just how much Melton meant to him. Pa's words, "It's right to fight for what is yours," came back to him. Marvel knew now Melton was like a brother. He would fight with all his strength to keep Melton safe. But for now it seemed there was nothing Marvel could do. He tried to get a look at his captor.

"Kay!"

Marvel puzzled over the Indian's word and decided it must mean no. He stared at the Indian's arms and compared them to his own. Their arms were about the same size, so were their legs. Marvel was sure this Indian could not be much older or taller than himself.

One question after another whizzed round and round in Marvel's head. Could these Indians be showing their courage by capturing them? He felt sure the Indians had been hunting. He could see a number of deer on one of the lead horses. Had the hunters seen their covered wagon and decided to follow it? Had they watched his father shoot the turkey yesterday and realized Pa was a good marksman? These thoughts sent chills up Marvel's spine. Yet, somehow, they filled him with pride. Pa, at least, was safe. What would he do? Marvel thought about the slow oxen and knew Pa would have to find a horse. But that would take time.

Marvel's thoughts wandered to Rags. He was sorry the dog had been hurt, but he felt better knowing he was sleeping in the wagon. These Indians carried bows and arrows. If Rags had barked at them, they might have killed him. If Pa found a horse, who would take care of Rags?

These questions made Marvel forget about his situation.

The group suddenly came to a stop near the top of a hill. The Indians talked in muffled tones about something in the valley below. Marvel studied all of them for the first time. Some of the fifteen were dressed in leather shirts and leggings. Most were boys wearing only breechcloths and moccasins.

Marvel wondered what was so interesting in the valley. Half of the Indians rode silently off in one direction, half in the other. Only the two braves with their captors and the deer-laden horse remained behind. But why? Marvel wondered. Then he saw a wagon and some horses hidden among the trees. He heard distant sounds of shooting, followed by hair-raising screams. Then silence. Marvel was afraid to think what that might mean as they waited. They did not wait long. The group soon returned with the stolen horses. Marvel felt sick when he caught a glimpse of the Indians sporting a fresh scalp. He knew from the look on Melton's face that he had seen it, too.

Once they returned, the Indians started out again. Marvel decided the two who turned back were checking to be sure they were not being followed. When they returned the party headed west.

Hour after hour, they traveled toward the sinking sun. Darkness was settling when they finally came to a stop near a creek. Marvel and Melton were thrown to the ground and promptly forgotten. The Indians watered their ponies and drank without a glance in their direction. The boys longed for food and water. They lay gagged and hobbled on the damp creek bank.

Melton heard a coyote howl in the distance. He remembered how frightened he had been when he first heard that sound. Now it was a friendly reminder that they were not alone. Finally, the two boys fell asleep.

Several hours later, two Indian braves picked up the sleeping boys and threw them roughly across the backs of the two ponies. Still stiff and sore from the previous day, Marvel moaned when the horses made their way through the uneven creek bed.

Melton's head throbbed with pain. He tried to think of a plan. "If my mouth wasn't covered," he thought bravely, "I would bite this Indian. And if I was untied I would punch him one." But Melton knew there was really nothing he could do but watch and wait.

In the bright moonlight he watched Marvel and his captor. The Indian's long, black braids were held in place by a narrow band. "He doesn't look old, but he sure looks mean," Melton thought as their two ponies trotted side by side. In that brief moment Marvel's eyes met Melton's. The younger boy tried to speak. Only a muffled sound came out.

The trees and bushes seemed different here. When Melton saw the tall cypress trees like the ones near Center Point, he thought of home. With a heavy heart he pictured his mother. Would he ever see her smiling face again?

10

The Search Begins

"Faster, faster, Cain and Abel! Go faster!" Pa shouted. "Can't you hurry up? Oh, I have got to find a horse or I will never rescue my boys."

Pa looked from the slow oxen to the sleeping dog at his feet. He thought for a moment that Rags was making up, but the dog settled back down. Finally, Pa found it impossible to sit still any longer. He took the rope from the side of the wagon. He tied one end loosely around the dog and the other and to the seat. Pa mumbled softly, "Sorry about this rope, but I have to tie you. I don't want you waking up and jumping out of here. I have enough troubles without that."

Pa jumped to the ground with his rifle in the crook of one arm and the reins in his other hand. He walked along with the oxen, thinking about his problems. The grisly picture of the Indians kidnapping his children kept floating before his eyes. Pa had never experienced so many emotions at one time: anger, frustration, helplessness and, most of all, fear.

He pulled the map from his pocket and studied it carefully. "It seems the only thing to do is to follow this river a few more miles and then turn north," he said aloud. "I reckon we are bound to come to a house or settlement by nightfall if you two will pick up your feet!"

Pa could not see the colorful butterflies fluttering among the bushes for his dismal loneliness.

"Now, John Sellers, it's not going to do any good to mope like this. So start making some plans. You need help if you are going to find the younguns!" After scolding himself, he kicked a rock to show his anger. A few minutes later he stumbled in a hole and almost fell.

"There, see what you get for not being careful? No wonder the Injuns got the boys. Now you listen here, Sellers, you start thinking straight. There is a right way and a wrong way to everything. One way is right as Christmas and the other is wrong as sin! Now make up your mind what it will be." He squinted at the sky and continued. "It must be about noon. Now, Cain and Abel, I reckon you need to eat and rest a spell. I must check that dog."

He stopped near the bank and, balancing the gun, took the bucket and filled it with water for the oxen. Once they were taken care of he turned to Rags. The dog was half awake. He whined when he saw Pa.

"I did a dumb thing. I let the Injuns get our boys! You're hurting, Rags, but I'm hurting too. Nothing can ease my pain, but there's no need for you to be hurting. My medicine lasts only a few hours. It must have worn off and that is why you're in pain. I will give you some more."

Pa put the medicine in the turkey the way he had before and offered it to the dog. "Here, Rags, eat this. While you are resting I will try to find a place to stop. Maybe you can stay there a few days while I go look for the boys."

Rags licked Pa's fingers, swallowed the turkey, and lay back on Marvel's coat. Pa turned to the oxen. "Come on, time is wasting. We have miles to make before night. Let's go north."

They turned from the main road onto a little-used trail. Pa soon discovered the bushes and undergrowth made travel more difficult. He hoped this path was a short cut to where he wanted to go. He knew from the map that the other road was better, but it was not the most direct way to the nearest settlement — New Braunfels.

Time passed slowly while the afternoon grew hotter. Insects buzzed around, tormenting the oxen and making them swish their tails and toss their heads. Pa's shirt stuck to his back. His feet hurt from walking on the rocks. Mile after mile he went in lonely silence.

Sometime later, Pa studied his map again. He whispered a prayer of hope, begging for help from above.

The land gradually flattened. The trees became sparse. The thick undergrowth of a few miles back gave way to knee-deep grasses. Pa skirted a deep gully and guided the team up a gentle, grassy knoll. Pausing to let the oxen rest, he scanned the horizon for some sign of people. Then he saw it — a house! His heart skipped a beat and he rubbed his eyes to be sure he was not dreaming. "It is a house and smoke! Come on, boys, you can do it." he yelled, quickening his own steps. "There is a house over yonder and there must be people because I see smoke. Come on. You can rest all night."

When they neared the cabin, Pa saw the rock fences and plowed fields. "This must be a German family. I understand they are good farmers. They are good people, too. I just hope they will help me." He yelled loudly, "Hello! Anybody home?"

A man suddenly appeared from the shed behind the house. He was carrying a bucket in one hand and a musket in the other. A large woman appeared at the doorway. She, too, carried a rifle as she dried her hands on her apron. The woman walked to the edge of the porch and watched Pa.

"Hello!" Pa shouted again. "Can you help me?"

"*Guten tag, herr.* Good day, mister. What is the trouble?" The blond-headed man walked to within a few feet of Pa. The two eyed each other for a few moments. The German extended his hand and clasped Pa's firmly. "My name is Hans Schmitt. What is the matter? You need help?"

"I'm John Sellers from Center Point. The Injuns kidnapped my boys back up the river. I need a horse. Can you help me?" Pa's voice was desperate.

The woman called to her husband, "Hans. Bring him to the house. Supper is ready. Mister, you are hungry, *ja*? Hans, he will want to wash."

"Thank you kindly, Mrs. Schmitt. I reckon I could eat something." The woman's friendly face reminded him of Ma and home. Pa followed the man to the washbasin on the porch. While he washed he looked at the house. It was bigger than Pa's house in Center Point, but it, too, had a breezeway between the two cabins. Pa suddenly realized how hungry he was when the delicious fragrances of home-cooked food drifted from the kitchen.

"Kinder, kinder ... children." Hans called while clanging the metal bar hanging at one end of the porch. Children appeared from the direction of the barn and field. One by one they stopped to wash their hands. Hans called each by name as they entered the homey kitchen to find their places at the long hand-hewn table. Pa thought of his own family back home as he counted the three girls. The four boys were older than Marvel. They had their father's clear blue eyes and blond hair, but their jolly, smiling faces were like their mother's.

Pa was sure nothing could be more beautiful than the hot, fluffy biscuits, brown gravy, and ham hocks swimming in beans on the table. He never knew he could be so hungry for a woman's cooking.

Hans encouraged Pa to tell his story while they were eating. The young people hung onto Pa's words. Visitors were rare, and a story like Pa's was especially interesting. Pa ended his tale by declaring, "So, you see, I need a horse. I'd like to leave my wagon and oxen till I can get back with your horse. Will you help?"

Hans looked at his wife. "Hilda, we help, *ja*? We let him take Ole — Ole is a fast horse. Carl and me, we ride to New Braunfels with him so he won't get lost. We get seeds for planting, too, while we are there. What you think, Hilda?"

His wife nodded in agreement. She turned to Pa to ask, *"Herr* Sellers, Mr. Sellers, you rest some days, *ja?"*

"No thanks, ma'am," Pa protested quickly. "But I appreciate the offer. You see, it's a long way to Goliad to get my brothers. I have to leave in the morning. But I will spend the night if you will let me. Oh — I almost forgot — I have a hurt dog in my wagon." The children's eyes brightened with renewed interest. "Poor critter got his feet burned in the fire. He will need to stay quiet until his paws heal. He will grieve for the boys. I reckon he had better be tied under the wagon or else he will decide to go looking for them. That is, if you don't mind keeping him until I can get back."

All of the children talked at once. Pa felt sure the German words meant they were begging to keep the dog. Pa laughed. "With all these youngsters, Rags will like it here. In fact, he might decide to stay." Pa sipped the steaming coffee slowly. "Ma'am, that's the best meal I have had in a long time. This coffee, too, is plumb tasty."

Hilda beamed with pleasure and smiled. *"Danke!* Thank you! If you have to leave, I fix something for you to eat. *Herr* Sellers, we keep your dog. *Ja*, Hans? But put him up on the porch so the children can watch him. Carl, get the lantern. Is dark out there. You help him with his dog."

Hans took the lantern from the shelf and lighted the wick. "Here, Carl, you carry this. We get his dog. Fritz, you find covers for the woodbox. That way he sleep better." The two older boys nodded.

The girls chattered excitedly as they did the kitchen chores while the boys fixed the box for Rags. Once he was in his new bed, poor Rags did not stay awake for long. He gave a mournful whine and closed his eyes. The boys were fascinated with the bandages.

Pa explained slowly. "Rags accidentally fell over a burning log when Melton was playing with him. That is how he got hurt. If we can keep him quiet a few days, he will be fine. He's a good dog, but he is always hungry."

When the Schmitts heard that, they offered him food. But Rags was not interested. For once he was too sleepy to eat.

Pa apologized. "I reckon he's still pretty groggy but, come morning, he will want to eat. You will see."

"So," Hilda said with a yawn, "is bedtime, children."

They protested until Pa smiled at them and said, "Would you like to tell Rags goodnight? He would like that."

One by one they filed by to pat Rags and, with a backward look in his direction, headed off for bed. When Pa told Hans and his wife goodnight, Pa thought wearily "tomorrow will be a better day."

11

With the Indians

The Indian ponies walked in single file down the twisting path. Marvel jumped in spite of himself when an owl hooted somewhere nearby. Then, to his surprise, one of the Indian riders answered the hoot.

The tall, leafy branches of the cypress and sycamore trees along the trail hid most of the canyon as well as the cliffs on the opposite side of the river. Marvel caught glimpses of the winding river far below in the canyon. Through the patches of green he could see many tents and knew they were the Indian tepees that Pa had described. The narrow path turned first this way then that in its descent to the valley. Glancing up to the way they had traveled, Marvel saw the path was lost in the dense trees and foliage.

When the ponies made one final twist near the floor of the canyon, the Indians began to whoop, *"Hea-heit,Hea-heit!"* (Hello).

Their cry brought the quiet camp to life. Indian women and children appeared from out of nowhere shouting, *"Hea-heit!"*

They followed the riders down to the water's edge. With much talking and laughing the braves slid from their horses and, sprawling flat on their stomachs, drank from the river. Marvel and Melton wondered what would happen next. They soon found out. They were thrown to the ground with a thud and, for the moment, the helpless boys were forgotten. There they remained while the men bragged about their adventures on the hunt. When no one was watching, Melton inched over to Marvel's side. Their fingers touched. Their eyes met. Tears of joy rimmed the younger boy's eyes. He was no longer alone.

Sometime later two of the Indians remembered the boys. One of them turned to Marvel, yanked him to his feet, and untied him. Marvel recognized those hands — he had stared at them for hours. In spite of the Indian's mean black eyes and grim unsmiling face, Marvel knew they were about the same age. He pushed Marvel's face into the shallow water. Marvel sputtered and choked. The Indians laughed at him. Marvel did not think it was funny. He slowly lowered his head to get a drink of the cool water. He never knew anything could taste so good.

The other Indian pulled Melton to his feet. His cruel eyes glared at him as he untied Melton and pushed him down. He fell at the edge of the river near Marvel. Melton lapped the water like a dog, enjoying the coolness on his throat. The clear water turned pink as it met the dried blood caked on Melton's face and head.

Their talk grew louder and louder. Listening to their voices, Marvel felt sure the Indians were bragging about their bravery and courage. Suddenly, the two Indians pulled Marvel and Melton to their feet. The women and children laughed and jeered at the boys as they stumbled toward the clearing. When they reached the fire, they stopped.

The Indians formed a circle around the boys and squatted to the ground. The frightened boys were shoved into the center of the ring. All the while, cold, unfriendly eyes glared at the boys. No one spoke. Marvel and Melton stared back. They were too afraid to wonder what could happen next.

A fat Indian woman wearing a buckskin dress stepped forward. She reached for a fistful of Marvel's hair and laughed in glee as his curls popped back into place. One by one the other women stood up to pull his curls. Everyone laughed. All the while they were saying *"Wer'se Pappy"* (Curly Hair). *"Wer'se Pappy!"*

Some distance away near the tallest of many tepees sat an elderly Indian couple. Their faces were wrinkled like dried leaves. Their eyes were dark and sunken. The old man stood and raised his hand. All were silent.

Though his voice trembled with age, the Indian spoke with authority. *"Wer'se Pappy,* Curly Hair . . . you!" He pointed to Marvel. "You *Wer'se Pappy,* You Curly Hair."

Marvel was surprised that the old man knew a few English words.

The large woman then turned to Melton and touched his white hair timidly. She whispered the words, *"Tip-e Pape, Tip-e Pape"* (Whitehead).

The others echoed her words. *"Tipe-e Pape, Tip-e Pape."*

The old Indian man pointed his bony finger at Melton and said. *"Tip-e,* squaw name you Whitehead."

A brief silence followed. Then, without warning, the people began dancing. They formed a circle around the boys while they chanted and danced heel-to-toe around them. They sang, *"Pappy, Pape, Pappy, Pape."*

The old man repeated the words, "Whitehead, Curly Hair."

Melton and Marvel knew they now had Indian names.

The crowd gradually wandered away. The women returned to their work. The children ran to play while the men gathered in groups to talk. The two boys found themselves alone. No one seemed interested in them now that their fun was over.

Marvel wondered if they had been forgotten. He looked around for a way to escape. But, before he could make a move, an Indian came up and pushed them into one of the tepees. The man then shifted the cords from the boys' wrists to their ankles, making sure they were securely fastened. With a grunt of satisfaction, the Indian walked from the tepee.

After being in the bright sunlight, the boys thought the Indian home was cool and dark. Once they were alone, Marvel threw his arms around Melton. With the ordeal they had been through, they laughed and cried at the same time.

Marvel sighed deeply and said, "I wouldn't have been surprised if they had killed us. Are you all right? When I saw that blood all over your face I was scared. You looked half dead."

"Oh, I'm all right, but that fellow made me mad! I will pay him back if I ever get a chance," Melton vowed angrily. "Just feel of my head. I have a couple of bumps as big as eggs, and I have a headache."

"Glory, that is as big as my fist," Marvel exclaimed when he touched the lumps. "But you will be all right, your head is hard."

Marvel fell back on the dirt floor to think. He felt exhausted from all that had happened — the long day's ride, fear of the unknown, along with his hunger. With his head resting on one arm and his other hand in Melton's. Marvel looked at the top of the tent. Tiny beams of light streamed through the crossed branches that gave the tepee its form. He could see where the thick hides were sewn together to make them large enough to cover the cone-shaped base. Marvel let his eyes travel to the door. It was made by folding back the outer edge of the hide.

"I wish Pa could see this. I'll bet he has never been inside a tepee."

"I wish I hadn't," Melton grumbled. "Speaking of Pa, I wonder what he thought when we didn't come back. Glory, we must have ridden a million miles or more. I'll bet Pa will never find us!"

Marvel leaned on his elbow to glare at the boy in disgust. "Don't you talk like that, Melton Sellers! You know Pa will try. In fact, I thought I heard his gun when we rode off. I've been thinking about what he will do. First, he will have to find a horse. He would never find us in that covered wagon."

"You're right. He could never find us with just Cain and Abel. But you're wrong, too. Pa will get a horse all right and he will get someone to help him look for us. He might get those Rangers he talked about or he might even go to Goliad for his brothers. I just bet he doesn't come alone. He will have somebody with him."

Marvel nodded. "You may be right. In the meantime, what are we going to do? Do you have any ideas?"

"Glory, yes — eat! But it seems we can't do that. There's nothing to eat. So, I reckon the next best thing is make a plan. The way I see it, we haven't much choice — hobbled like this." While he talked, Melton had been working to loosen the cords that bound his feet together.

Marvel also pushed at the knots, but he was unable to move them. He finally gave up in disgust. "You are wrong about one thing. We can eat!"

"What? Dirt?"

"Nope. Don't you remember we put corn bread and turkey in our pockets for Rags? I've got the turkey. Have you got the bread? We had best save some of it, they might not feed us for days."

"Glory, don't say that. I'm half starved now!" He pulled the flattened bread out of his pocket and shook his head. "There sure isn't much here."

"A little is better than nothing," Marvel declared, taking the two thick slices of turkey from his pocket. "They may forget to feed us."

"Forget on purpose," Melton moaned. "Well, here goes. We'll take a bit of turkey and bread and save the rest. How about that?"

"Fine." Marvel agreed, biting into the crumbly bread. They ate slowly trying to make it last longer. Marvel glanced out the doorway. "I wonder what time it is? Looks like it's almost dark."

61

"I don't know." Melton's voice trembled. "Marvel, do you miss Pa?"

"Now, don't you start crying. We have to be brave. We can't let them see us crying and moping around. Injuns don't cry, remember?"

"Humph, I'm not an Injun." Melton sniffled.

A dark shadow of a woman appeared in the doorway. A strong odor came from the bowl she carried in her hand. By the fading light Marvel recognized her as the first woman who pulled his hair. She placed the bowl at their feet without saying a word and vanished into the night as silently as she had come.

Melton sniffed the bowl. "That sure smells peculiar. Do you think she's trying to poison us? I'm almost too scared to eat it." He touched the hot meat and licked his fingers. "It taste strange, too, but I reckon it is better than starving to death. I guess you know we haven't had a full meal since yesterday morning!" Melton bit into the meat and gagged at the taste. "Glory, what is this stuff anyway?"

Marvel tore at the chunk of meat with his teeth, grumbling. "Whatever it is, it sure is tough. It must be deer. I reckon it's best that we can't see what we are eating. Pa always said Injuns don't cook their meat much."

Melton moaned with his mouth full. "Oh, don't say that!"

When the bowl was empty, they pushed it toward the door with their feet and stretched out on the ground. A spooky hoot of an owl came from somewhere close by. It was followed by the mournful howl of a coyote. Melton shivered.

"That is just a lonely critter talking to his friends. Don't be scared." In the blackness of the tepee, the older boy sighed. "I reckon we had better go to sleep. There is no telling what those Injuns have got planned for tomorrow."

12

A Ride for Help

The tantalizing aroma of coffee blended with spicy sausage drifted into the room where Pa was sleeping. As the fragrance reached him, his nose twitched and his eyes flew open. He sat up and tried to unravel his jumbled thoughts. "First things first," he mumbled under his breath. He walked to the porch to check on Rags. The empty bowl near his box told Pa that the dog was almost back to normal. Rags wagged his tail when he saw Pa, but he was content to stay in his box.

Pa stood up and breathed in the clean, fresh air. He noticed the dew drops on the red and yellow flowers growing near the porch and heard a noisy mockingbird in a nearby tree. He whispered softly, "It will be a good day."

The sound of voices came from the kitchen. When he entered, Pa found Hans and his family waiting for him, with breakfast ready to begin.

"Gunten tag, Herr Sellers."

"Good day to you, too," Pa replied. "But please call me Doc — everyone else does."

"Breakfast is ready, Doc. Sit down." Hans pointed to the empty chair at the end of the table.

While one of the girls poured the coffee, Pa admired the food on the table. He could not wait to eat one of the golden biscuits when the plate was passed his way. He was hungry.

"Mercy, this looks good, Mrs. Schmitt. It sure beats my burned bacon and corn pone. I'm not much of a cook." He licked the melted butter from his fingers as he talked.

"Thank you, *danke*," Hans's wife said with a wide grin. "Please call me Hilda. You a doctor, *ja*?"

Between bites of sausage and biscuit Pa nodded his head.

"My Hilda's a smart woman!" Hans said clearing his throat. "Last night she figured a way to find your boys. Me and Carl go with you to New Braunfels and help you find a Ranger. Maybe Ranger help you look for your boys. Then we — Carl and me — ride to your brothers in Goliad." The family waited eagerly for Pa's reaction to that suggestion.

Pa looked from one to another slowly. It took him a moment to find his words. "You mean you would do that — for me — a stranger?"

"*Ja.*"

Pa found it hard to control his voice as he spoke. "I thought that I had died and gone to heaven when I smelled your cooking, Hilda. Now I know I did!" The children giggled at his words. Pa went on. "Glory — that's what my Melton says — isn't this something? Why didn't I think of the Texas Rangers myself?"

Hilda refilled his empty cup and smiled. "The dog is better, *ja*? He was hungry like you said. Is good, no?"

"Is good, yes! And I feel like a new man. What a breakfast — what a day! I'll bet I could whip an Injun with my bare hands — well almost." They laughed at Pa's joke.

"While Carl and me get the horses, my Hilda fix us food. And, Doc, is good you make map of way to Goliad and write letter to your brothers, *ja*? We take it with us." Hans put the paper and feathered quill with the ink on the table in front of Pa and turned to his family. "We go to work now."

Hans and his boys headed for the barn while the women busied themselves in the house. Pa listened to their chatter as he copied his map for Hans and wrote a note of explanation to his brothers. He no longer felt afraid. He now had a plan and a horse. Could it have been only yesterday, he wondered, that he lost the boys? It seemed like an eternity.

Pa was finishing the map when Hans returned. He went out to check on Rags and change the bandages while Hans talked to his wife. The Schmitt boys came up to watch Pa. He explained each step of how to apply the medicine. Pa was glad to see the dog's paws were healing. The boys nodded their heads as Pa told them to keep the Rags tied up. They understood he might wander away looking for Pa and the boys.

The rosy light of dawn filled the eastern sky as Carl led the horses to the house. He handed Pa the reins of the largest one. "This is Ole. He is the fastest."

Pa rubbed the horse's soft nose and, with thoughts of Ma and his own children, was eager to be on the way. He did not have long to wait. Once their bedrolls were tied to the back of the saddle, they were ready.

"Is time, *ja*?" Hans announced with a wave of his hand.

Pa found it difficult to put in words what he was feeling. "Thank you, *danke*, Hilda, for everything. I will be back as soon as I get my boys. Goodbye."

"Auf Wiedersehen, and good luck," Hilda called. "And, Hans, you and Carl be careful."

Everyone waved and shouted farewells at once as the three rode away. Pa could not help remembering Ma's farewells and thinking about how different things had been that day. The horses left a cloud of dust behind them as they headed off down the road.

The scenery changed to low scrub oak trees scattered among the weeds and grasses. They traveled sometimes three abreast, sometimes in single file. All the time the sun was creeping higher and higher in the sky. Pa knew these horses could travel in an hour what it would take the oxen a day or more to cover.

And so, sometime later, Hans pointed to the right.

He said, "Doc, we'll be there soon. New Braunfels is just across the river."

After traveling a few more miles, they came to the river. The horses splashed through the clear water and up to the bank.

"That was the Guadalupe River, Doc," Carl said with a smile.

Pa pictured his wagon near the Guadalupe with Devil's Backbone in the background. What a difference a day had made.

13

The Texas Rangers

New Braunfels was the largest town Pa had seen in years. He looked from the signs written in English and German, to the school and churches down the street. There were so many covered wagons and buggies he could not count them all. He stared at the shoppers. They started at him. Pa could not help admiring the long, swishy gowns and feathered hats some of the women were wearing. Remembering Ma's homespun dress and faded bonnet, Pa wished he could buy her material for a new dress, but his pockets were empty.

Hans said, "New Braunfels has four mills, seven wagonmakers, and two shoemakers. Is a busy place, *ja?*"

Pa nodded, looking around for the baker that he knew, from the delicious fragrance, was somewhere nearby. It was just down the street. He muttered, "I reckon I'm as bad as Melton, always thinking about food."

When they stopped and tied their horses to a hitching post in front of a building marked *Zeitung*, Pa puzzled over the word. "This is our newspaper office," Hans explained proudly. "We have a paper a week—just like in Germany! Is good? They want news for paper. We tell about your boys. The news of the town is here. They will know where to find a Ranger."

When they entered the printing shop, the musty odor of ink and newspaper greeted them. An attractive young woman looked up from her work and smiled. *"Guten tag."*

A gray-haired man in an ink-smudged apron turned from his desk and smiled. "*Guten morgen*. May we help you? I am Ernest, the editor. That is my daughter, Hertha."

Hans felt more comfortable in his native language. He spoke in German as he told Pa's story. He repeated it the way Pa had told it to him. When Hans paused to catch his breath, the editor glanced in Pa's direction and smiled understandingly. Although Pa did not know all Hans was saying, he heard the word "Rangers." The girl's excited gestures and pointing led Pa to think she knew where they were.

"*Danke*, thank you," Hans said, turning on his heels. Carl and Pa followed him to the door. They exchanged handshakes and farewells with the editor and his daughter and walked out to the street. "We have luck. There are two Rangers at the blacksmiths. We go there," Hans said as they mounted their horses.

They rode back through town past the church and the school. Most of the shoppers had gone home. Only a few people were on the street. Two sleepy horses waited patiently for their owners near the baker's shop. When they came to the blacksmith shop they stopped, hitched their horses, and walked inside.

The shop seemed especially dark and smoky to Pa. It took him a minute to adjust to the light and clanging noise. The smithy was hammering hot, glowing metal to make a horseshoe. He worked until the edges were smooth, then plunged it into a tub of water. The red-hot metal made a sizzling sound.

When he was finished, the smithy looked up and dried his sweaty face on his sleeve. "*Guten morgen*! Good morning — you need shoes, no?"

Hans smiled. "No, *danke*. But we need Rangers. Is here, *ja*?"

"*Ja*, sleeping." The smithy pointed toward an open door at the end of the building. "They there," he said, returning to his work.

With Hans in the lead the three men walked toward the light and on outside. Pa's eyes traveled from the two

68

double-barreled shotguns to the two men stretched out on the ground. He studied them closely like a doctor examining a patient. They wore scarred leather leggings, runover heeled boots, and sun-bleached pants. Each had Colt six-shooter pistols and a supply of ammunition in the holsters around his waist. The cowhide cuffs on their wrists were well-worn. Both had a rawhide lasso fastened to the saddlebags beneath their heads. Hats partly covered their unshaven faces. Their unkept hair poked out in all directions.

Pa felt satisfied with what he saw. "Those two look like a couple of wild buffaloes — rough and tough," he mumbled under his breath. "If my boys can be found. I reckon these are the fellows who will be able to do the job."

The two men slowly pushed their battered hats back on their heads and, with scarcely a move on their part, Pa found himself looking down into a loaded pistol aimed at his head.

"Don't shoot, Mister," Pa pleaded. He and Hans lifted their hands into the air.

The Ranger with dark hair grumbled jeeringly. "Why not? What do you fellows want, anyway? Can't we get any sleep? You almost got your heads blown off by sneaking up on us like that. Didn't they, Henry?"

"Sure did!"

"We didn't mean to scare you. My name's Sellers — John Sellers from Center Point. And this is Hans Schmitt and his son Carl. I need to talk to you."

The Ranger seemed to relax. He replied, "I reckon you didn't know any better, so put your hands down. What do you want, Sellers?"

Pa squatted to start his story. When he came to the word "Injun" the Rangers were on their feet. Pa stood up, too, to finish his explanation. "And my friends here have agreed to go to Goliad to get my brothers."

The Rangers exchanged glances. The dark-haired one said. "There isn't any need for that. There are wagons from the shingle's camp coming through here going to

Gonzales every few days now. We'll get word by them to your brothers. If you can write you can send a letter. That way your friend here can go back home. His family might be needing him if there's trouble."

Pa looked into the cold, blue eyes of the Ranger who had spoken and replied, "I can write."

The Ranger ignored Pa's words. He went on talking. "My name is James — he is Henry. And if you want the truth, Sellers, you must be plumb crazy!" Pa clinched his fist and blinked but — before he could speak — the Ranger continued. "There is talk of war everywhere — what with the North arguing about slaves and the Injuns getting all riled up. That is why Governor Houston sent word for folks to stay near their homes. You sure did a dumb thing, Sellers, starting for Goliad with two younguns that aren't dry behind the ears." James shook his head in disgust.

"Now, James," his friend said slowly," it's too late now. Sellers, where did you say you lost your boys?"

Pa felt relieved at the chance to escape James's cold, criticizing gaze. He took out his map quickly and placed it on the ground to point to the spot he had marked. "It was about there by the river, near Devil's Backbone."

"Did you see which way they headed? How many were there?"

"Well," Pa rubbed his chin thoughtfully, "there must have been ten — maybe more. They headed west."

The Ranger named Henry chuckled. "You are lucky that our horses needed shoeing, Sellers. We are heading west once we leave here. Come on, let's see about our horses. We will leave a message for your brothers with the smithy. He can send it by the next wagon drivers going toward Goliad."

James gave Pa a scornful look and said, "Sellers, there really isn't anything your brothers can do. They have troubles of their own what with the Injuns acting up. You had better let us Rangers handle this our way. We know what to do without your help."

70

Pa was normally a peace-loving man, but he decided the time had come for him to set things straight with this Ranger James. He stood on tiptoe to look eye to eye with the man and cleared his throat. With eyes as frightening as a rattler's and in his deepest, deadliest voice, Pa spoke. "Mister! Let's get this straight right now. My name is *Doctor* John Sellers and I have not seen my brothers in almost ten years. I figure I am as smart as the next fellow — that includes you. As far as I am concerned, if I want to go to Goliad, that is my business! Now, as I see it, we have got a job to do — you and me — and that is to find my two boys. So, we will put aside our feelings for now. I am going with you Rangers, do you understand?"

The Ranger's grim expression slowly softened. A broad grin crept across his unshaven face. Ranger James threw back his head to bellow a laugh that shook the ground where they stood. He slapped Pa's back with a whack that almost knocked him off his feet. James roared, "Why didn't you say so in the first place, Dr. Sellers? You are just the kind of fellow we are looking for. Isn't he, Henry? You have gumption and brains. Yes, sirree! Doc, You are welcome to come along and help us look for your youn-guns. Glad to have you."

Hans looked from one to the other and whispered hoarsely, "Doc? Is trouble, *ja*?"

Pa relaxed and smiled. "Nope, just a manly agree-ment, Hans. Now — as I understand it I will give this," he produced the letter from his pocket, "to the smithy. He will give it to the next wagon driver going to Gon-zales. Then it will get on to Goliad. Is that right?" Ranger James nodded. "So Hans, you and Carl had better go back home. This fellow says Hilda might be needing you if there is trouble with the Injuns."

Hans chuckled. "My Hilda can outshoot and outfight three men! My girls, too. Carl and me go with you if you want us, Doc."

Pa put his arm lightly around his friend's shoulder, "Thank you, *Danke*! I know you would go, but I don't

71

want you and your boy maybe getting hurt for my mistakes. You all run along home."

In their brief friendship Pa had grown to appreciate Hans's simple goodness. He shook hands with them and wondered when — or if — they would meet again. "I will be seeing you. If I'm not back, for some reason, in a month would you get word to my wife in Center Point?"A lump formed in his throat as he added, *"auf Wiedersehen, goodbye, my friends."*

Pa turned his back to prevent their seeing his tear-rimmed eyes and mounted his borrowed horse. Hans's farewells faded in the distance as Pa followed the Rangers along the Guadalupe River. He knew they were traveling the very road he and the boys should have taken if they had not followed the Kirks' advice and crossed the river. Pa wondered if he would still have the children if he had stayed on this trail. He muttered, "Now, John Sellers, what is done is done."

Pa hated to admit it — even to himself — but that Ranger was right. He had done a dumb thing putting his boys' lives in danger. But Pa knew if there was a way he would find them.

In his heart he puzzled how — in a place as big and wide as Texas — anyone would know where to look for two young boys.

14

The Fight

The next morning the boys were awakened by the sound of Indian voices. They had trouble at first remembering where they were or how they had gotten there. Then Marvel moaned softly, "I wonder what they are going to do with us?"

"I don't know, but I'm not scared — not much."

They stared at the patch of sunlight around the roof of the tepee. Suddenly, they realized they were not alone. The woman who had brought their food the night before placed another bowl on the ground and picked up the empty one. Without saying a word to the boys, she again vanished as quickly as she had appeared.

Once she was gone Melton reached for the bowl and looked inside. He wrinkled his nose in disgust. "This smells awful! It doesn't look so good either! It's burned on one side and bloody on the other. Ugh!"

"It must be bad if you're not eating it" Marvel teased. Secretly, he had to agree that it did look pretty awful. He closed his eyes and forced himself to take a bite. He could eat no more.

A short time later the man who had tied them up reappeared at the doorway. He squatted on the ground to unfasten their ankles. Melton stared at the jagged scar on the side of his face. The man pulled them to their feet and shoved them out the door. The boys were too frightened to hear the birds or to see the butterflies floating lazily in the nearby weeds. They could only wonder what was going to happen to them. They soon found themselves in the center of a circle with Indians all around. They recognized the old man who had given them their names. An Indian twice his size sat on his right.

Marvel could not help staring at him. He wondered if he was the chief of the tribe.

The large man rose to his feet and said something to the two Indians who had captured the boys. They pointed their fingers at Marvel and Melton, crying, "*A he!*"

Marvel mumbled the words to himself and somehow knew they meant "He's mine," or "I claim him."

Nodding his head, the chief sat down and crossed his arms. With that signal the two young Indians suddenly leaped to their feet and sprang toward the white boys. In spite of his fear, some sixth sense told Marvel he had to do something — anything. He could not just sit there and not fight back.

"Run, Melton, run!" With those words the two were off and running. The Indians were right behind them. Round and round they went. There was no way for the white boys to escape.

Suddenly, they heard the old man shout, "*Pappy — Pape*, fight, fight! Run faster!"

The boys understood his meaning. Although they were smaller and weaker than the Indians, they knew they could outrun them if they tried. Melton swerved to one side, causing one of the Indians to stumble and fall. The Indian sprang up to meet Melton face to face. Melton surprised him by bending low to run between his legs. The onlookers around the circle made a deep, guttural sound to show their approval of the move.

Out of the corner of his eye Marvel saw Melton's actions and made up a few new ones of his own. He confused his opponent by turning and twisting to double back. The old man's words of encouragement excited Marvel. He was determined not to give up without a fight.

Melton swerved to the right and meant to double back, but the Indian chasing him blocked his plan. He grabbed his arm and flipped Melton over his shoulder. Melton found himself sprawled at the old man's feet and felt his hand on his head. Melton was too stunned to move. For some reason he did not understand, the fight for him was over. The old man had come to his rescue.

Meanwhile, Marvel wondered how much longer he could evade his enemy. He wanted to drop in his tracks but instead managed to keep just out of reach. The Indian lunged, ripped Marvel's shirt from his shoulder, and grabbed his hair. The chief stood to his feet and raised his hand. As suddenly as it had started, the fight was over. The chief pointed his long finger at the snake's rattles hanging on the string around Marvel's neck.

Marvel stared spell bound at the yellow feathers entwined in the man's black hair and at the long shells dangling from the top of his ears. There was a strip of brown leather around his head, and two long braids hung down his back. The neck opening of the man's fringed shirt revealed a bear claw necklace. Marvel felt sure this man was the Indian chief when he said something Marvel did not understand, Marvel looked to the old man for help.

The elderly Indian said, "*Pappy*, Curly Hair, snake . . . you kill snake?"

Fingering the rattlesnake necklace around his neck, Marvel trembled with fear. "No," he said, "my Pa killed the snake or I would be dead."

The old man smiled. "Your Pa . . . he brave. You, *Pappy*, brave." With those words the old man got slowly to his feet to talk to his people. Was Marvel imagining it, or did the unfriendly faces soften as the old man spoke? The chief asked a question and looked around the circle. His question was answered by a show of hands. "You, *Pappy*, live — for now." With those words the old man walked slowly toward his tepee.

The boys found themselves being shoved into a tent different from the one where they had spent the night.

They knew it belonged to the old Indian. He was sitting cross-legged at the doorway.

An elderly woman sat cross-legged on a buffalo rug just inside the entrance. Her short gray hair hung limply about her ears. She wore a leather pouch around her neck. Her thin body was hidden by the loose blouse and fringed buckskin skirt that lay in folds on the rug.

Marvel whispered, "There's something wrong. You think maybe she is blind?"

Melton watched her for a moment before he crawled toward her. As he drew near, the woman turned her head in Melton's direction and, jabbering excitedly, reached out to touch his hair. The boys did not know the man was watching them until he spoke.

"She Moonbeam. She no can see. *Cda'ma woon'ie* — she see you, Whitehead. You stay here, with her. Be eyes. She my woman — squaw." With those words the Indian returned to his spot outside the tepee.

When the squaw finally took her hand from Melton's head, he crawled back to the center of the tent with Marvel. "What do we do now?"

"I don't know. It seems she is almost blind, but she sure likes your hair. Maybe that is what saved your life and somehow these saved mine." He toyed with the rattlesnake necklace while he talked. The air was warm from the sun beating down upon the tent. Marvel yawned sleepily. "I'm sure thirsty. If they hadn't hobbled my legs, I would try to find us some water. Say, you don't suppose they forgot about us, do you?"

"I hope not. I'm starving! Let's eat the bread and turkey that is left." Melton did not wait for an answer. He was hungry.

Once the last crumb was gone, Marvel pulled his harmonica out of his pocket. "Do you remember the fun we had with Pa? He always said music makes a fellow feel better. Why don't we see if that is true? Let's sing that song Pa taught us. Ready? One . . . two . . ." On three the tepee was filled with music. The woman was startled at first by the racket. But after a few minutes she began to clap along with the tune. It was not long before the old man joined them.

The Indian children had been playing outside the tent, but the noises from inside aroused their curiosity. One by one they left their game of "grizzly bear" to follow the sound. Before long the tepee was crowded. The old Indian stood up and pointed toward the door. The Indian children ran outside and formed a circle on the ground.

"You go out—all see. You—Curly Hair—make music." He turned to Melton. "Whitehead, you out. Help Moonbeam. I—" he pointed to himself, "Black Wolf go out."

The man helped Melton to his feet. With Moonbeam's hand on his white head, he repeated his words. "*Pape*, Whitehead, help Moonbeam."

Melton had no choice but to guide her unsteady steps toward the light. Once they were in the open, Black Wolf looked at Marvel. "You play, Curly Hair." The Indian children made room for them in the circle.

Marvel took a deep breath and put the harmonica to his lips. The more he played, the stronger and louder his music became. Marvel forgot his fears and began to enjoy the song he was creating. The onlookers clapped and chanted along. When he paused to catch his breath, Marvel saw the women crowding around. They shouted, "Shaunt!" (Good).

Black Wolf got to his feet and raised his hand. A hush fell upon the group. "*Pappy* Curly Hair, you good— *shaunt*. They say you good. Me, Black Wolf—peace chief— say you good. You stay here."

The Indian faced his people. As he talked they listened respectfully. They had selected Black Wolf for the peace chief because of his great wisdom and goodness. His words had been their law for many years. They chose the war chief of their tribe for his bravery and courage as a warrior. The war chief was their leader only in battle. Black Wolf was their leader of wisdom. When he spoke, they obeyed.

Now Black Wolf had spoken. One by one they moved away. The white boys found themselves alone with the elderly couple again. Moonbeam's eyes sparkled against her leathery skin. She patted Melton's head, muttering, "*Woonie, woonie*" (See you.)

"Marvel, do you think she sees my white hair?"

Black Wolf answered the question. "Yes, Moonbeam see you. You stay. I keep. You no run away. Me teach you Indian ways. No run." He began to untie the cords around their ankles.

The boys knew they were now free, but what did it mean? What could they do? What would the old Indian teach them? Could they run away? Where would they go? Which way would they run? But the most important question of all — where was Pa?

These questions were quickly forgotten once Black Wolf started their lessons. He showed them feathers from a buzzard, a turkey, and an eagle. They soon knew how to identify each one. Black Wolf taught them to make a bow and arrow. During one lesson, the old Indian drew picture symbols in the dirt with a stick. The boys quickly learned to read each one — two figures meant friends, a moon was a month, and a sun meant one day. After that lesson, Black Wolf had them read the symbols painted on his tepee. He was pleased the boys could read them without his help.

"That's a dead bear," Melton exclaimed proudly.

"And there is a rattlesnake."

"Glory! Isn't this something! We are learning to read Injun!"

Marvel wondered what his father would say if he could see them. He remembered Pa's words, "A fellow does what a fellow's got to do." Marvel was sure Pa would understand. They had no choice but learn about the Indians and their ways.

15

Tracking the Indians

Pa sighed. He was thinking of his boys. There was Marvel — so alive, so eager. He always jumped and asked questions later. Perhaps some day Marvel would be a doctor if that was his real ambition. But Melton was different. The boy was serious, solemn, thoughtful. What were his dreams? He never spoke of them. He accepted each day as it came. Yet, under it all, Melton was curious and perceptive. Something about the boy reminded Pa of a bottomless pool of water. Melton's words often showed a wisdom beyond his years.

Life to Pa was precious. Each second was important. He knew there was a time for everything: a time to sow, a time to reap; a time to laugh, a time to cry; a time to live, a time to die. Surely this could not be the time for his boys to die. They were so young, so full of spirit. They had their whole lives in front of them.

Suddenly, Pa realized the two Rangers had left him far behind. They had warned him that they might when they mounted their horses back at the blacksmith's shop. Ranger Henry had said, "Don't expect us to poke along, Sellers. We've got to catch up with the patrol down by the river. That's where they said they would wait for us. So we will be making tracks. Come on!"

Pa saw they were not joking. They expected him to keep up with them. Pa knew his borrowed horse was fast, but the Rangers' horses were faster. They were half wild and swift as the wind. Their hooves looked like windmill blades on a windy day. Those frisky ponies fairly flew over the ground. They knew how to avoid the deep ruts and chug holes caused by the heavy wagons and the recent winter rains.

Pa rode hard to catch up with his companions. Suddenly, one of them made a deep croaking noise like a frog. Someone in the distance echoed the sound. Pa knew that was a signal that they were near the Ranger camp. When they stopped at the river to water their horses, Pa washed the dust from his face.

The men unfastened their saddles and turned their horses loose to graze with the others. Pa dropped his gear beside Ranger Henry's and followed him to the fire.

"Howdy, James. What took you fellows so long?" James mumbled somthing under his breath.

Pa looked at the group. He counted fifteen in all. He could not remember ever seeing a more wild bunch of men. Most were unshaven, and none were too clean. Pa knew he did not look much better. He noticed a second fire a short distance away. When he saw a small band of Indians huddled nearby, Pa tightened his grasp on his gun.

"They're our scouts," Ranger Henry said. "Just relax." Pa was not sure he would — or could — relax until he found his boys.

"Sellers, that's Captain Jones, our leader," Ranger James said.

Pa nodded. Before he had a chance to speak. Henry spoke up. "Fellows, this is John Sellers — *Doctor* John Sellers. He's got a problem and needs our help, but I will let him tell you." All eyes focused on Pa.

He squatted beside the fire and took the steaming cup of coffee someone put in his hands. Pa cleared his throat before starting his story at the beginning. When he finished, he paused. Then, with a half-hearted grin in James's direction, he added, "I reckon I made a mistake starting for Goliad in a wagon with my younguns. But there wasn't much talk of war with the North in Center

Point. Besides, folks seemed to think the Injuns had quieted down. Of course, I figured you fellows had put those Injuns on reservations in Oklahoma." He glanced toward the scouts.

The captain rubbed his chin. "That's the trouble. We put them on reservations but they won't stay. I reckon they don't like being hemmed up. Some Comanches and Kiowas sneaked away and, of course, there are some we never did catch in the first place. Now they are like a swarm of bees around a hive. We never know when they will hit — or where."

Pa studied the man as he asked, "What is the answer?"

"Well, both the army and Governor Houston sent orders for us Rangers and the soldiers to help settlers when there is Injun trouble. We are patrolling between the Guadalupe River at New Braunfels and on up west."

"The Injuns that took my boys headed west."

"You are lucky, Sellers. We're riding that way come morning."

Pa mustered his courage to ask. "What do you think they will do with my boys?"

"It all depends. Sometimes they scalp them on the spot — especially the little ones that cry and scream for their Mamas. They kidnap girls and work them like slaves unless a brave takes a liking to one and wants to marry her. Almost anything can happen to boys."

Pa whispered hoarsely, "Like what?"

"Well," the captain drawled out his words slowly, "you never know what a party of Injun braves will do. They might kill them or they might trade them off for horses. They might even make them blood brothers. If that happens, I reckon them would become Injuns, too."

Pa gulped. He did not like any of those choices. He glared at the fire trying to gather strength for his next question. "What will the Injuns do if we catch up with them?"

The Ranger turned his head to spit a stream of dark tobacco juice into the weeds before he answered. "It depends." He did not finish his sentence.

81

Finally, unable to stand the suspense any longer, Pa demanded, "On what?"

"On lots of things. If we find them in camp with their women and younguns, they might just kill your boys! Or they might forget them in the excitement. If we catch them far from camp, they could let the boys go. You just never can tell for sure what will happen." He stopped.

"So?"

"So, come morning we will head for Devil's Backbone. I understand that was where you lost your boys. Is that right?"

Pa heaved a heavy sigh of relief. "Near there. But that was three days ago. You think we can still pick up their trail?"

"We will give it a try, Sellers. But I reckon we had better get some sleep. We will have a hard day tomorrow. Say, who's going to take the second watch?"

"It's my turn," someone grumbled sleepily.

With that settled, the men turned in for the night.

Pa stared at the sky. Finding his boys would be like finding one star from the hundreds above him. As he stretched out on the soft grass, many questions came to mind. How could they find the trail? If they did, what would the Indians do? Where were the boys tonight? Were they still alive?

16

Trail of Blood

The next morning it was pitch dark when Pa opened his eyes and looked around. Most of the Rangers were already up and about. He joined the ones heading for the river to wash. When he returned, the captain handed Pa a cup of thick black coffee and said, "Morning, Sellers. How about making a map here on the ground to show where you think you lost the boys?"

"I've got this," Pa said, pulling the map from his pocket. He laid it between them near the fire. The others stretched their necks to watch. Pa pointed to a spot on the map. "It was about there near the river, not far from that Devil's mountain."

Captain Jones studied the drawing carefully. He turned to his men to explain his plan. "Boys, we will cross over the river and cut northeast. We'll try to pick up the trail over there. Once they took the Doc's younguns, those Injuns probably headed west. Come on, break camp. Let's ride."

With the command, the group put out the fire, picked up their gear, saddled and mounted their horses. Riding two and three abreast, Pa and the Rangers crossed the Guadalupe River as the sun began to rise. Up ahead of them Pa caught glimpses of the scouts on their spotted ponies. He wondered how the Rangers could tell the friendly Indians from the savage ones. They all looked alike to him, except for the clothes they wore. The scouts, like the Rangers, wore rugged pants and shirts, not the leather breechcloths. Pa understood why; the prickly bushes and thorny limbs kept sticking into his legs. He wished for a pair of their leather chaps to wear over his pants. He mumbled, "I may not die from these scratches, but they sure do hurt."

The men had little to say. Each was lost in his own thought. Sometime later Pa had the feeling they were nearing their destination — the spot he had marked on the map. Then he saw the ashes of the fire where he had cooked the turkey. There were still feathers to remind him of that last meal with the boys. He shouted, "Hey, this is the place!" Pa could have saved his breath. The Rangers were already searching around the area. They knew where they were without Pa's help.

The sharp-eyed scouts quickly found an enamel cup Pa had dropped in his hasty departure. They followed the trail down to the river bank. There they located the spot where Melton struggled with the Indian. It did not take them long to find where the boy's boot prints stopped. Hoof prints pointed them toward the grove of trees. As the scouts headed that way the Rangers tagged along. Pa saw their interest in a low branch and knew they had found something. James yelled. "Sellers, there's blood on these leaves. One of your boys has been hurt!"

Pa felt anger, frustration, but — most of all — fear. He shook his head and stared at the leaves. How could the Indian scouts see things his inexperienced eyes overlooked? They wasted no time on the leaves. They were already searching for more clues. Suddenly, the scouts paused to look at a branch on an agarita bush hanging over the trail.

James cried, "We've found blood here, too, Sellers."

Like dogs on a scent, the scouts picked up the trail again and headed northeast. They rode single file through the thorny undergrowth and cactus plants, zigzagging all the while, searching for clues. On and on they went. Mile after mile the party followed the trail. The icy feeling around Pa's heart began to melt because he knew they were going in the right direction.

Sometime later they came to a river. The horses picked their way down the steep, rocky bank into the muddy water. Pa hoped his boys had not tried one of their foolhardy tricks. He knew Marvel was often too daring for his own good. Besides, neither of them were good swimmers.

Once they crossed the river the Indian trackers found the trail again. Even Pa could see the now familiar unshod hoof prints on the soft dirt. They had traveled for some time when they found another low branch caked with blood. They found strands of Melton's white hair caught on a twig.

The group stopped at the edge of a hill to wait. The scouts had ridden into the valley below. Pa wondered what they had seen down there. He soon had his answer. James hollered. "There's a covered wagon behind those trees. A man has been scalped. His horses are gone."

Pa tightened his grip on Ole's reins, mumbling under his breath, "Why, that could have been me and the boys down there!"

There was little doubt in any of their minds but that the kidnappers had done the killing and stolen the dead man's horses. They now had two kinds of hoof prints to follow — shod and unshod.

The afternoon sun was sinking in the west when the scouts circled back to the group and stopped to talk to the captain.

"Men, we will camp here," Captain Jones announced a few minutes later. "Let's unsaddle and build a fire for coffee. I don't know about you, but I could eat a bear. Take a look around and see what you can find to eat."

At the thought of food Pa remembered Hilda's supply of biscuits, dried meat, and sausage she had put in his saddlebag. "Captain, I don't have a bear, but I'll share what I have. It won't be much, but you are welcome to it."

One of the men found a bush loaded with berries to add to the meal. They sprawled around on the ground near the fire to enjoy Hilda's cooking. A short distance away at a second fire, the Indian scouts took dried deer meat from their packs and ate in muffled silence.

"Sellers,"the captain said. "This is where those Injuns stopped the first night with your boys. As best we can tell you, there are about fifteen of them. We can't find any boot markings near here or signs of a fire. I reckon that means your boys didn't get any water or supper that night. But at least we think they are alive—or were then."

Pa did not feel like talking. He walked to the edge of the group and sat down. A howl from a coyote reminded him of their first night away from home when he had assured the boys they were safe. How wrong he had been. Would they ever be safe again? Pa fell asleep thinking of Ma. What would she say if she knew her boys had been taken by Indians and that Pa was chasing across the country looking for them?

17

The Powwow

Far above the canyon basin the bright sun peaked through the thick layer of leaves that overshadowed the Indian camp. The boys watched the scar-faced Indian enter the tepee and whisper something to Black Wolf. The two left without saying a word to Moonbeam, who sat in her usual position near the door. The boys were surprised that Black Wolf had left so abruptly.

"I wonder what that's all about," Marvel mumbled.

"I don't know. But, Marvel, I was thinking about Pa. Do you miss him? I sure do," Melton's chin trembled.

"Of course I do, but it won't do any good to cry. We ought to be glad we are learning Injun ways. Who knows, they might come in handy some day."

Melton wiped his tears on his sleeve and swallowed the lump in his throat. "I am glad, but I keep thinking about Pa — and Rags — and Ma. How long have we been here anyway? It seems like forever."

"Well, let's see," Marvel began. "The first day was when the Injuns got us. I've been thinking we could have been more careful, but it is too late now. Anyway, we rode all that day. Remember?"

"Not really. All I recall is that Injun hitting me on the head. I can't remember much else. Seems I do recollect crawling over to you that night when we finally stopped. Glory, I was thirsty and scared. I wanted to cry."

"Yeah, me too." Marvel pictured Melton's bloody face. He sighed. "That was the first night. Yesterday we rode in here and got our Injun names."

"Was that just yesterday?" Melton grinned sheepishly as he said. "You know I think those women liked my white hair, don't you? Did you see how they looked at me?"

"Maybe they thought you were a ghost," Marvel teased, "or maybe that you were a pretty girl!" He ducked as Melton playfully tried to box his ears. "So this is the third day and what a day! I never did understand why they stopped fighting, did you?"

Melton shrugged his shoulders and looked up. Black Wolf had reentered the tepee without a sound. He lifted two fingers and said, "*Pappy*, pony — two."

"What?"

Black Wolf repeated his words. The second time he pointed to Melton and lifted two fingers. "*Pape,* pony — two."

"I think he's telling us he bought us for two ponies!" Black Wolf smiled and nodded his head. Melton went on. "Now, doesn't that beat all? He bought us! For two ponies! Wait until Pa hears about this."

The old man motioned for them to follow him. "Come, *Pappy, Pape.*"

The boys fell into step behind him. They squinted their eyes from the bright sun and looked around. The women were working on the ground by the fire. Black Wolf signaled for the boys to move closer.

The squaws were beating pieces of raw meat with stones. Once it was tender, they added berries and continued beating the mixture. When it was thin as paper they molded it into long rolls and put them on poles near the fire.

"That pemmican. Dry . . ." Black Wolf held up eight fingers toward the sun then bent toward the fire and wiggled his fingers.

"I'll bet that means it dries by the fire for eight days," Melton said. The Indian smiled and beckoned them to follow him. When he stopped to speak to a group of other old men, the boys read the symbols on one of the tepees.

Melton looked back at the Indians and said, "Do you suppose they are talking about the old days? That's what the men do when they get together in Center Point."

"Maybe. Just think — when we are old we can talk about our life with the Injuns. That is, "Melton's voice faltered, "that is, if Pa ever finds us."

"Now, you know Pa will find us — if he can. Besides, who will believe we learned Injun writing and how to talk with our hands?"

When Black Wolf finished visiting with his friends, the boys walked with him to the river. The Indian put his finger to his lips and pointed to the footprints in the soft mud. The boys recognized the skinny prints of a bird, but what were the others? A sudden movement in the shallow water caught their attention. They looked up in time to see a turtle slip from a rock into the water. A short time later they saw his head appear downstream.

Suddenly, they heard the sound of many horses in the distance. Black Wolf sighed heavily. "We go. Me go *powwow.* " He pointed three fingers skyward.

"You are going on a *powwow*? For three days?" From the chief's face Marvel knew he had guessed correctly.

"What is a *powwow*?"

"Don't you remember? Pa called that a meeting."

"You . . . *Pappy, Pape* . . . you stay. Moonbeam see you." The old Indian lifted ten fingers and added the sign for boy. "Teach you ride. Run . . . arrows." When they did not understand, Black Wolf repeated his message.

"Melton, he means Moonbeam needs you. Ten boys will teach us to ride and run from arrows."

The Indian smiled. "*Shaunt* . . . good. You good Indian, *Pappy*. We go."

Retracing their steps, the boys knew from the sounds that something was different before they reached the camp. The women and children were chattering excitedly. The men had painted their faces. Their ponies had red circles painted around their eyes. With faces like stone the Indians waited for Black Wolf. Once he was seated on his horse he looked at the boys. With scarcely a movement he winked at them before his pony fell into line behind the others. The men rode single file up the path. The men who were too old to travel watched them sadly. The women and children called excitedly, *"A-ya, Ki-i-hah"* (Goodbye). Everyone waved until the party disappeared from view at the opposite end of the canyon.

Moonbeam stretched out her hand. *"Pape? Pape? Cda'ma woon'ie* . . . Pape? See you . . . see you . . . ." The woman placed her hand on Melton's head. The two boys looked at each other wondering what they should do. There was nothing to do but stay with Moonbeam until Black Wolf returned. But what was going to happen? Where was Pa? Would he ever find them? If so, when?

18

Rescue

Pa's first thoughts the next morning were of his boys. Were they somewhere nearby? He rubbed his whiskers and yawned. By the light from the campfire he saw several sleepy-eyed Rangers heading for the creek. He joined them.

"Morning, Sellers," James called when Pa walked up. "Coffee is ready. Do you want a cup?"

"Morning," Pa replied. He squatted by the fire and reached for the cup. One of the men handed him a corn cake. Pa washed it down with the black coffee. The food tasted like his own cooking — sort of burned.

"Men," Captain Jones looked from one to another while he talked. "The scouts think we are getting close. We will wait until it's almost light, then we will move. So check your guns. Get ready for a fight."

Pa's chest throbbed. The moment he had waited for — yet dreaded — was at hand. He cleared his throat. "Captain, is there danger of my boys getting hit if there is going to be shooting?"

"Sellers, I told you from the beginning you never know about the Injuns. Anything can happen. A lot depends on your younguns and what has happened since the Injuns took them."

The captain paused to bite into a hunk of tobacco then replaced the package in his pocket. He continued. "Understand, Sellers, we Rangers usually ride without stopping. That means we ride night and day if we are tracking like this. We eat what we have without bothering about a fire. Of course, with you along we didn't want to lose the trail. We have been going slow and easy. But this is about to change." He turned to his men and gave his usual command. "Come on, let's ride."

Pa's bones moaned as he settled in the saddle. He could think of many reasons he would not be a Ranger — riding night and day was one. Eating whatever he could find was another reason. He longed for Ma's home cooking. This morning even the thought of his own scorched bacon sounded good. "Glory," he mumbled in disgust, "I *am* getting to be like Melton — always thinking about food."

They moved quietly through the thickly wooded area. Pa recognized the cypress and sycamore trees, but the others were new to him. It was difficult to see the Rangers for the dense foliage and underbrush. Pa caught a glimpse of one scout who rode back to speak to the captain. The Ranger leader raised his gun to give a signal to his men. Pa's throat went dry — the moment had come. With rifles ready, the men moved forward silently. Pa was not far behind them. When they reached the clearing the captain stopped. What Pa saw made his blood run cold. Five Indians were shooting arrows, and Marvel was their target!

With only a leather shield to protect himself, the boy had no choice but to run. His only defense was to hold the shield before his body for protection from the flying arrows. On a signal from the tallest Indian, Marvel was forced to run to the nearest tree and then retrace his steps with the arrows flying all around him.

Before Pa could make a move to help his son, he saw Melton. They had loosely strapped him onto a wild horse. The boy clasped the animal's mane to keep from falling off. Melton's face was deathly pale.

The Indians were laughing and shouting so loudly they did not hear the Rangers until it was too late. The white men were upon them before the Indians knew it. The Rangers' guns went into action. Two braves fell on Marvel, knocking him off his feet. The three went down together. The other Indians ran in all directions. The Rangers were right behind them.

Pa raced for his boy, who was still clinging to the wild horse. Bullets whizzed past him. The noise of the guns caused the half-crazed animal to rear up on its back legs and Melton's body flew through the air. Somehow Pa managed to catch him before he fell. He let Melton's body slip gently to the ground.

Wheeling his horse around, Pa looked for Marvel. He found him half buried under two dead Indians. With the experienced hands of a doctor, Pa quickly examined the boys. He was relieved to find that although they had a number of cuts and bruises, they had no broken bones. The boys were dazed and bewildered by all that had happened so quickly.

While the other Rangers were seeing to the Indians, James and Henry rode back to check on Pa. "How about it, Doc, are your boys all right?"

"Yes, Henry," Pa said, "but it was a good thing we got here when we did."

Marvel sat up with his father's help and stared at the lifeless Indians beside him. With a shudder he put his head on Pa's shoulder. "I knew you would come."

Melton threw his arms around Pa's neck, crying, "We knew you would find us."

Captain Jones and some of the other Rangers had returned to be sure the boys were safe. "Well, men, it seems the Doc has what he wanted." The captain paused to clear his throat. "I reckon we had better get out of here before the whole tribe comes down on us. Let's ride."

"Young fellow," Ranger James said reaching down for Melton. "How about riding back with me?" Melton was too tired to protest.

Pa lifted Marvel to his horse and jumped up behind him. He grinned sheepishly and yelled, "Let's ride, men."

Zigzagging around the low hanging branches, the horses and their riders flew like the wind, retracing their steps through the grove of trees. They sped past their previous campsite without a backward glance. The animals, like the men, were eager to leave the Indians far behind. On and on they rode.

93

Sometime later they came to the muddy river that they had crossed the day before. The captain shouted, "Men, we have ridden hard. We'll let our horses rest a spell." The others stopped to let their horses get a drink. Captain Jones looked from the children to their father. "Sellers, the scouts have been watching to be sure we aren't being followed. It seems we are safe for now."

Ranger James rubbed his chin thoughtfully. "It is strange that those Injuns didn't give us a chase. We sure made enough racket."

Melton's eyes twinkled. "Pshaw, I could have told you they wouldn't follow us if you had given me a chance. There are only women and old men left in camp."

The men stared at Melton. "How do you know that, boy?" Henry demanded.

Melton grinned impishly. "Black Wolf—that's the chief—told us! He and the other Injuns left yesterday for a *powwow*."

Henry threw back his head and laughed. "Well, I'll be! If that don't beat all!"

The captain chuckled, too. "Sellers, I'd say your boys took care of themselves. I don't know why you were so worried!" Everyone laughed. "Well, in a few more hours we will be back to Hans Schmitt's place. We ought to be there by dark. You can get your wagon, Sellers, and we will ride with you part way to Center Point. That is, unless you still want to go to Goliad."

Pa moaned softly. "Captain, all I want to do is get my wagon and go home. I'm plumb tired of traveling! I just don't know how you Rangers live like this."

The men laughed.

Suddenly, Marvel declared loudly, "Pa—you didn't think the Injuns were trying to hurt us, did you? They were only teaching me to run from arrows! And they were teaching Melton to ride a horse."

The Rangers stared at the child in disbelief. They waited to hear what the doctor had to say about that.

Pa shook his head. "Son, there is a right way and a wrong way to learn. Would you pick up a rattlesnake and say, 'Mr. Rattler, you wouldn't bite me, would you?'"

Marvel's eyes rolled at the thought. Pa went on. "Well, there is a right way to learn to ride a horse, and throwing a little boy on a bucking bronco isn't the way! Why, Melton could have broken his neck. Do you understand?"

Marvel looked shocked. He realized his father spoke the truth. "Glory, I never thought of that!"

Pa moaned. "And what could you learn with them shooting arrows at you? Why, they outnumbered you five to one! An arrow could have hit you leg or, if you had dropped that shield, you could have been killed."

"But, Pa," Marvel protested, "they were laughing and having so much fun!"

Pa shook his head in disgust. "Son, folks sometimes laugh and enjoy another fellow's hurts and pains. I reckon they just don't know any better!"

The Ranger thought about the doctor's words.

James cried, "Like I said before, men, that Doc's got brains and gumption! Why, he might have gotten himself killed with all of our shooting, but he only thought about his boys. Now, I call that being a real man!"

Melton grinned. "That's my Pa all right. He is some man!"

Pa's face turned pink. "Shucks, a fellow does what a fellow has to do. That's all."

Sensing his father's embarrassment. Melton teased, "Glory, Pa! We knew you would come. But what took you so long?" His eyes twinkled mischievously. He grinned at Pa.

The Rangers laughed. Henry jeered, "Yeah, Pa, what took you so long?"

Marvel looked at his father's tired face and patted him understandingly. "I'm with you. All I want to do is get my dog and go home to Ma — and her cooking!'

As they rode into the muddy river, Melton yelled, "Glory, Pa! I'm hungry!"

Bibliography

Juvenile

Beatty, Patricia. *A Long Way to Whiskey Creek*. New York: Morrow, 1971.

———. *How Many Miles to Sundown?* New York: Morrow, 1974.

Hoff, Carol. *Johnny Texas*. New York: Dell Publishing Company, 1950.

———. *Johnny Texas on San Antonio Road*. New York: Dell Publishing Company, 1950.

Hofsinde, Robert (Gray Wolf). *Indian and His Horse*. New York: Wm. Morrow, 1960.

———. *Indian and the Buffalo*. New York: Wm. Morrow, 1961.

———. *Indian Picture Writing*. New York: Wm. Morrow, 1959.

———. *Indian Sign Language*. New York: Wm. Morrow, 1956.

Place, Marian (Templeton). *Comanches and Other Indians of Texas*. Harcourt, Brace, 1970.

Richard, J. A. *Under Texas Skies*. Austin: Benson, 1964.

Warren, Betsy. *Indians Who Lived in Texas*. Dallas: Hendrick-Long, 1981.

Adult

Bennett, Bob. *Kerr County Texas, 1856–1956*. San Antonio: Naylor, 1956.

Davis, John L. *The Texas Rangers; Their First 150 Years*. San Antonio: Institute of Texan Cultures, 1975.

Fahrenbach, T. R. *Comanches; the Destruction of a People*. New York: Knopf, 1974.

Green, A. C. *The Last Captive*. Austin: Encino Press, 1972.

Hagner, Lillie Mae. *Touring Texas Through the Eyes of an Artist*. Waco: Texian Press, 1967.

Kilgore, Daniel. *A Ranger Legacy; 150 Years of Service to Texas*. Austin: Madrona Press, 1973.

Kownslar, Allan. *The Texans, Their Land and History*. New York: McGraw-Hill, 1978.

Lord, Walter. *A Time to Stand*. Lincoln: University of Nebraska Press, 1961.

Newcomb, William Wilmon. *The Indians of Texas*. Austin: University of Texas Press, 1961.

Phares, Ross. *Texas Tradition*. Gretna, La.: Pelican Press, 1954.

Reading, Robert S. *Arrows Over Texas*. San Antonio: Naylor, 1960.

Schreiner, Charles. *A Pictorial History of Texas Rangers*. Waco: Texian Press, 1969.

Sheffy, Lester. *Texas*. Dallas: Banks Upshaw and Co., 1954.